D0383778

Gerry leaned in with his patented look of concern. "Is everything all right?" he asked me.

I had just made three Banana Splitsvilles in a row. They were works of art, as far as I was concerned. You have to stick flags with toothpicks through banana wheels and then into each scoop of ice cream, and arrange coconut and chocolate flakes in perfect symmetry with chopped pecans and walnuts, and then there's the whipped cream. I mean, it could take some people three or four minutes. I've got it down to two and a half.

"Everything's fine," I said.

"Really." He gazed into my eyes as if he were about to tell my fortune. "Everything's fine at home."

I nodded.

"At school."

I nodded again.

"With Dave."

I tried to nod, but my neck got stuck in this cramp all of a sudden, and I couldn't get it to move. So instead I smiled, showing him all my teeth.

"You've been snacking on the pecans again," he said.

Busted.

Books by Catherine Clark

CATHERINE CLARK

Banana Splitsville

HARPER TEEN

An Imprint of HarperCollinsPublishers

HarperTeen is an imprint of HarperCollins Publishers.

Banana Splitsville
Copyright © 2000 by Catherine Clark
All rights reserved. Printed in the United States of America. No part
of this book may be used or reproduced in any manner whatsoever
without written permission except in the case of brief quotations
embodied in critical articles and reviews. For information address
HarperCollins Children's Books, a division of HarperCollins
Publishers, 1350 Avenue of the Americas, New York, NY 10019.

www.harperteen.com

Library of Congress catalog card number: 2007929412
ISBN 978-0-06-136715-1
❖
Revised edition, 2008

For Bart "Woo" Scherer,

wherever you are

Acknowledgments

Thanks to Elise Howard and Abby McAden for their inspired editing. Thanks to Ted Davis for believing in this project so strongly and many thanks to Shannon Daut, Carmen Manning, Wendy Scherer, Sally Suhr, and Harold Winters.

How hurt do you have to be to sue for emotional distress?

Do you have to be completely devastated? Or can you just be extremely mad?

What about "really, really pissed off"? Does that hold up in court? I need to call *Judge Judy*. I need to be *on Judge Judy*. She'd rule in my favor. She would. After I made a devastating case against him. Which I think would be easy, even though I haven't exactly gotten into law school yet.

Is it bad form to drink a diet Squirt at 9 in the morning?

Well, I don't know, and I don't care. I don't even know why I'm writing this down—I don't keep a diary. But I have to jot this down—for history's sake. The History of Jerks.

Nothing I do could be in as bad form as what Dave did last night. I haven't even slept. Well, except from 4-8.

I can't believe I'm about to write this down. Dave actually broke *up* with me.

Broke up with *me!*

Sorry if I'm writing in really bad form, what Mr. Arnold calls "choppy" in my essays. But I feel a bit chopped up.

What was even worse than the fact he dumped me was how he did it. So tacky. Over the BBQ, while I watched my veggie burger burn, tempeh breaking down

1

into flames like my life. I invite him over for a cookout, so we can plan how we're going to move all his stuff to Boulder next weekend. And he has a soda and some chips and then proceeds to tell me he's going to move on with his life now, thank you very much. Like I'll ever be able to eat again. He comes to my house and does this. Doesn't he know anything about how to break up with someone?

Oscar was running around the yard, yelping, like he does before a big thunderstorm and during fireworks every July 4th. Animals can *sense* these kinds of things coming—why didn't I?

What follows is actually what he said. I'm not making this up. I wish I were.

"We'd probably break up in October anyway, so we might as well do it now, start the year free and clear."

Free and clear—that's like a *deodorant*, right? No, wait—that's a cell phone plan. Are you listening to the words coming out of your mouth, I wanted to say. Do you realize you are rhyming really offensive words, like "year" and "clear"?

"Yeah, and we'll probably die one day, so we might as well kill ourselves now," I said, following his brilliant logic.

"Courtney. Don't be like that," he said.

"Me? You're going to tell me how to be now?" That was when I got a little hysterical. Like he had the right to stand there and calmly eat barbecue-flavor potato chips and tell me my personality needed work. He's about as sensitive as a day-old hamburger bun. Which I wish I had served him. Maybe with nails inside the bun. He had orange-red powder on his lips from the chips and a speck or two on his soul patch. I was going to make fun of him, but I started thinking really depressing things like how I'd never kiss him again.

Then he thought he was getting through to me, because I was crying. So he went into his "this is really for *your* benefit" speech. "It'll be so different, with me away at college, I don't want to burden you or hold you back—"

"You're the one who doesn't want to be held back!" I said. "You don't want a high-school girlfriend. You want to go to frat parties and pick up girls—"

"I do not!" he said. "That's not why I'm doing this at all."

"Then why *are* you breaking up with me?" I said.

Ha. He didn't have a comeback for that.

But unfortunately I got caught up in staring at him while I waited for his comeback and I realized he was wearing that T-shirt I bought him when we went on that trip to Phoenix and Taos last spring and it's all faded now and looks really good on him because the washed-out blue kind of matches his eyes. And I got so furious at him for being able to look good while being such a jerk that I told him to leave.

"I'll call you," he said.

"Don't," I said, indignantly, like you're supposed to. Then he drove off, just like that, and I started bawling like a two-year-old. Okay, like *Bryan* when he was two years old.

People warned me about this. Said it might happen. Alison (supportive big sister as always) said we *should* break up, because "that kind of relationship never works."

"What *kind*?" I said.

"Long-distance," she said.

"He'll be in the next town," I said. "It's a half hour *drive*. When the traffic's bad." From Denver to Boulder is nothing, people do it every day as a commute. They have buses on the half *hour*. Crowded ones. And we even live slightly on the west side of the city, which is that much closer. He could get here by bike, even.

"Same thing. You're not in school together anymore. It wouldn't work."

Well, sure, it definitely wouldn't work *now*. After all the stupid things he said, about how we needed to grow and how we might find out we wanted to get back together, but we'd cross that bridge when we came to it.

I'm not crossing that bridge. I'm not even looking for it on a map. As far as I'm concerned, I was on that bridge, and he cut the rope on the other side, and now I'm hanging over a raging river, and people are going by in their kayaks and laughing at me. You know, those people who are really good at kayaking and never take off their sandals, not even in the winter. I hate those people. I think kayaks should be banned, except that extremely buff guys seem to paddle them bare-chested a lot.

I have to go back to school in a week. Ugh. Everyone's going to ask how my summer was, and I'm going to have to tell them me and Dave are over. That's so humiliating. Couldn't he have waited until October break or something? His timing sucks. Just like everything else about him. I can't believe what he did, I can't believe him. I'm never going out with another guy again. At least not for a long long long time. Mom doesn't care about men. Why should I?

Anyway, Dave's whole position is just so absurd. Alison, college girl, actually tried to *explain* his viewpoint. What does Alison know about relationships? She hasn't even had one since first grade with Timmy What's-His-Name.

Of course, she did sit up talking with me and Beth until 2 A.M., and she did go out and buy Ben & Jerry's Chocolate Fudge Brownie for us (which I technically don't eat anymore) (yum). We asked her to go, since Beth was so upset she was afraid if she went, she'd buy a pack of cigarettes. (She never gets asked for an ID. She's looked 20 for the last 3 years. Must be nice.)

Jane kept calling and we put her on speaker phone so she could join in the Dave-bash. Dave and I have been together for over a year. A whole year. Twelve months. We met last summer, and we were like John Travolta and Olivia Newton-John in *Grease*, only I have straight reddish hair and would never wear Spandex pants. Plus we fell in love in the summer and we didn't break up when school started. (At least, not *last* year.) And we didn't sing.

Anyway, now he wants to forget the whole thing and

"move on" and "grow," like a transplanted house plant in fresh soil. Mom tries that all the time. Each one *dies*. That's why she has the world's largest rock garden. Rocks, she can grow—or steal from national forests.

I hate plants.

I hope he gets replanted in that expansive soil that houses sink into and disappear. I hope he gets . . . what's that thing where you try to save water in your garden? Zeroscoped . . . xeriscaped . . . whatever. No water for Dave.

Mom and Alison left for Oregon today. I am supposed to be taking care of Bryan.

Like I'm not depressed enough.

Why is it so easy to write the first entry in a diary—and so hard to write the second? Is it because you read over what you wrote the day before and realize how dumb you sound? You tell yourself that you should never write in a journal when you're upset, because it ends up being so embarrassing to read it over. But the only time you really want to write in a journal . . . is when you're upset.

It's like a trick that blank book companies came up with. We keep grabbing for them, spilling out our guts, then getting embarrassed and throwing them out because we can't go on with page 2. Then we get upset three weeks later and buy another blank book and do the same thing. Total conspiracy. So forget it, journal industry. I'm not giving in, no matter how dumb-looking and dumb-sounding this is.

I could just . . . rip *out* the embarrassing pages, maybe. But that would probably ruin the binding. I'd really like to tear off the cover, except it's great camouflage because no one would ever guess this is mine. It's this disgusting pink-and-blue floral rose corduroy thing. *So* not me. It was a gift from Grandma Callahan (a Von Dragen by birth), who's still trying to feminine-ize me after all these years—like a pierced belly button with a small silver hoop isn't feminine.

Anyway, this book has about ten lines per page. Like I write that big anymore, like I'm a seven-year-old. I've already run over seven days with the first entry. That's okay; last night felt like it lasted a week.

Of course this style comes in handy on days when I don't want to write anything. Like, today.

Panicking about school. Contemplating calling in sick to Bugling Elk. For the entire year.

Home schooling works, right? People get into college from home schools.

Dropping out. Is the stigma really that bad? I mean, tons of kids do it, right?

I didn't tell Mom the whole story. She hates men enough already. I told her breaking up was a "mutual decision."

That wouldn't explain why I was bawling while I watched *The Serengeti Scene* tonight. Lions, tigers, Dave. Oh my.

Oh crap.

Okay, I've figured out what I need. A new diary=a new attitude. Will throw this one out as soon as I get through this. Which, as much as I'm writing lately, won't be long.

Whatever I just said doesn't make any sense. Another reason to throw this out soon.

I'll buy a cool sketch book with a black cover so it looks like I am drawing or only writing brilliant thoughts that don't require lines because they come so fast and furiously.

Alison called me tonight. She's settled into her new dorm room at Stafford and she likes everything and Mom is on her way back.

There was this really loud music and high-pitched screaming in the background. I kept asking her what was going on and she said, "Oh, nothing."

???

Since when does Alison hang out listening to loud alternative music with screaming girls? She hates them. She's supposed to be in like the conservatory or something. Playing concertos. Duets. In like . . . adagio. With a candle burning on top of the grand piano.

Then Dad called. Same old story from Phoenix. He's loving life and loving Sophia. Then he said he was very excited about becoming a grandfather soon.

"Don't push it, Dad," I said. "I just told you that Dave and I broke up. Alison's perennially single, and Bryan is *so* not ready."

He laughed and said he wasn't talking about *us*, he was talking about his stepdaughter, Angelina, who's having a baby in December, didn't he tell us?

Dad never tells us stuff and always thinks he has. It's chronic. Like when he was moving out.

(Sorry, but that still makes me mad.)

Angelina is only 17! And I'm not being judgmental, but I just can't imagine being a parent right now. I can barely take care of a dog. Do you give babies their pills in hot dogs, too?

Three days until school starts. Back to Bugling Elk High. Or, as I like to call it, Bulging Elk. I keep staring into my closet, as if there are answers in there, as if there are clothes I like in there. As if Dave's hiding in there.

I can't walk down the same bulging halls, sit at the same table we always sat at, listen to the same stupid bells ringing between classes. Also, after considering every item in my closet, my outfits suck. I'll need to focus more on outfits this year. Apparently I'm *single* now. I need to find dates and stuff.

Or not.

Beth and I had the same shift at Truth or Dairy this afternoon, masterfully mixing smoothies. Today was my day to be dairy and her day to be truth. I hate those days, because I guess you could say I'm pretty lactose intolerant. Or just sort of generally intolerant.

I want to be truth every day, but let's face it. Sometimes I'm dairy.

Anyway, I was stuck wearing the vinyl black-and-white Holstein apron; she got to wear the natural hemp one. I made 4 sundaes, 6 cones, and 3 milk shakes; she made 6 fruit smoothies, a soy shake, and she scooped up a dish of rice ice cream. Then she could tell I was depressed enough, and so she switched aprons with me. I thought that would cheer me up, but it didn't. Nothing could.

"Dave wasn't going to be here this year anyway, right?" Beth said while we were at T or D and she caught me staring at my reflection in the chrome base of the blender. The smoothie I was making got pulverized into tiny atoms, so thin and runny you could see through it, and I had to start over with another Sunrise Strawberry Supreme.

"You were going to miss him anyway. So now you'll just miss him . . . more."

"Beth," I said, "I'm never going to cheer up if you keep talking about stuff like that."

"But you should be sad," she said. "You need to be sad. You have to go through the phases of grief. See, first there's denial, then anger, then—" Blah blah blah.

She kicked into self-help mode. When she wanted to quit smoking, she went out and read every book and watched every show on getting over just about anything. She could probably be a psychologist with like two weeks of additional college courses, or at the very least give Oprah a run for her money.

Of course she only smoked for like three months, but she was really into it. Personally I think she just liked the boxes.

And she hasn't done too much about her addiction to boys, but I guess it's more important to quit smoking. For her, anyway.

"What you have to do, Courtney, is go for some sort of closure."

I flipped the sign on the front door of T or D before we locked up. "Like this? Closed?"

"See, that's what I'm talking about. Denial," Beth said.

Has he called? Like he said he would? No. I half expected to see him at Truth or Dairy today. He's sort of addicted to Coconut Fantasy Dreams. We both are. It was like . . . our drink.

Half expected. Whole-not-surprised when he wasn't there. I was all ready to give him the cold shoulder, easy to do when working around ice cream at Truth or Dairy all day. I could give him a really bad ice-cream headache, maybe, mix in extra ice in his smoothie and freeze his brain.

Like he could be any colder.

Dave moves to Boulder today.

I hate him.

The thing about breaking up with someone (okay, the thing about being *dumped*) is that your whole life just sort of . . . sucks. No, actually I was going to say that it *stops*. Dead end. (Don't worry, I'm not getting morbid here. Not much, anyway.) It's just . . . you thought you were going one way. And then the road just sort of ends, and you're staring at one of those yellow signs with a big arrow pointing in two directions and you have no idea which way to go.

The way I drive, I'd probably flatten the arrow. Head off into some farmer's field. Crush a few rows of corn. Maim a prairie dog.

How did I ever get started on this? Oh yeah. The breaking-up thing.

Like I really want to write more about *that*.

I think *I'll* start smoking.

It's true: life *can* get weirder.

There's this woman who comes in every day at 3:40. Well, every day I work, anyway. Even on Sundays. She does a shot of wheatgrass juice while she stands by the window looking outside, like she's either running from the law and wants to take off when she sees the police cruiser coming—or waiting for a bus that's really late, like maybe the route was discontinued a few years ago and nobody told her. She has wild, long frizzy brownish white hair. She wears really long skirts. And she has this bag. It's purple velveteen with silver swirls. Like something Merlin should have.

I call her Witchy Wheatgrass Woman. Not to her face, of course—just to Beth. I also abbreviate that to "WWW," as in "www.insane.com." She's the one who got Gerry to start giving out punch cards for one free wheatgrass with every ten purchases. Bluck. If you can drink ten ounces of wheatgrass, you should get a free *car*.

At least making wheatgrass juice is sort of satisfying, putting it in the little grinder thing and smushing it down. Something you'd like to do to a certain person named Dave.

After she does her ounce of green juice, she crushes the cup with her left hand and comes over to the counter for a water chaser. Everyone else says "water back," but she has her own term. Most regulars *don't* get water back, but then she's more like an "irregular," or maybe a factory second.

Then she talks. And talks. "A blue streak," Gerry says, although for her it should really be a green streak.

Today she felt like giving me advice on my love life. I guess I was saying something about missing Dave, and Beth was telling me the only way to get over him was to see someone new. Like how when she quit smoking she started chewing gum. Etc. Anyway, I think WWW only stands by the window so she can pretend she isn't listening to our conversations. I'm telling Beth—no more talking while she's in the store.

"To tell you the truth." She always starts off this way. Then sometimes she kind of laughs and says, "I'll get to the dairy later," only she never does. I don't know what the dairy would be—lies?—but. There you have it.

"To tell you the truth, I was never one for relationships."

Oh. Really. I dropped my scoop. Not in shock, but in shock that she felt the need to state the obvious.

"But if you have to have one . . . Courtney . . . " She always peers at my name tag, as if it changes on a daily basis. "Please. Practice safe sex. *Promise* me."

Oh my God. Why do all these people feel like they can give me advice all of a sudden? So she's health-conscious. So am I! Ice cream hasn't touched my lips in months. Well, okay, weeks. A week and a half, definitely.

But she annoyed me so much that I did a shot of hot fudge in retaliation. Don't tell me how to live my no-sex-life. Celibacy. Whatever. Free and clear of sex.

Came home and did yoga to relax. Didn't relax. Instead I stayed up late watching this *Our Mammals, Our Selves* program. Was starting to feel warm and fuzzy seeing all that video of baby animals, then made the mistake of switching to Animal Planet. That vet show was on. Surgery. Blood everywhere.

School in August? Does this make sense to anyone else? It's 90 degrees. We're sweating. My cool new sweater is wasting away on the shelf.

Made it to homeroom. Nobody seems to know about the breakup yet. Which might explain why everyone keeps asking me how Dave is. "Dead," I wanted to say. "With any luck." Maybe that was a bit harsh. I don't want him dead. Just temporarily maimed. Maybe by a wolf, or possibly a bear or mountain lion. If they can roam into the outskirts of Boulder, lounge in people's trees, and knock down their fridges, they can find Dave. It'll happen eventually. I just have to have faith.

I figure if I keep my head down and keep writing all day, no one will bother me. They'll think I'm psycho, but they won't bother me. Not sure which is the better way to kick off the school year. Reputation for being psycho, or fielding questions about my relationship. Or lack thereof.

I realize I may be psycho and also boyfriendless. And if so, I'm at risk of being a stereotype.

LATER THAT SAME DAY ...

The word is out. Apparently Dave felt like telling all his friends before he left town that it was time for him to be Free 'n' Clear (maybe not a deodorant—maybe a zit cream). They must have helped him with his brilliant lines.

So I went to the caffy for lunch (why? You may ask. Well, I figured it's that old story about getting back on the bike after you crash, or was that the horse? But mentioning horses and cafeteria food in the same sentence is a little scary), because Beth and Jane talked me into it, and because I was almost sort of hungry for the first time in a few days. I was trying to decide between the veggie taco and the peanut butter sandwich when it started. This murmur behind me. Like a wave of water. I thought maybe it was because I had picked up a taco shell to smell it, and it was kind of close to my ear, so I listened to it for a while as if it were a seashell, but all I could hear was grease soaking into my hand. I put it on my tray and grabbed a sandwich. But I could still hear the rushing sound.

I turned around and saw Grant Superior, one of Dave's best friends, who I used to think was nice, in this semihuddle with a bunch of other guys. All seniors. These guys huddle a lot, like they're attached. Three of them glanced over their shoulders at me at the same time. They are so unsubtle, it's scary.

I tossed my sandwich back onto the tray, and it

glommed back onto the pile. "Excuse me?" I said, walking toward them. "Was there a question?"

"Oh, uh, hi, Courtney," Grant said nervously. "We were just talking about . . . uh . . . "

"You and Dave. Splitting up. He says you hate him. Is that true?" Tom Delaney asked. He's so sleazy we call him "the Tom," as in "the tomcat." Constantly on the prowl. "'Cause if you guys aren't together anymore, I would really love to take you out sometime." He tried to put his arm around my shoulder.

"Yeah. Right," I said. "That'll happen."

Then I put my tray back. The idea of lunch after that was really rude.

Grant came up to me at the end of the day in Life Issues—this dumb new elective we have to take as seniors, it's supposed to teach us stuff that's not taught at school—hello, does anyone see the contradiction here? We're taking it *in school*.

Mr. Antero passed out the curriculum. It has things on it like "Coping" and "Moving On" and "Deal with It." Totally useless.

Anyway, Grant said he was sorry about the Tom being a jerk. I said, "We're *all* sorry about the Tom."

Grant laughed and started telling me how he'd talked to Dave and how it was too bad we split up. I cut him off. The last thing I want is sympathy from some good-looking guy about some other really good-looking guy.

After school Jane, Beth, and I went for our yearly first-day-of-school splurge. Well, okay, so it only started two years ago when Jane moved here from LA.

New lipstick, new nail polish (not tested on animals, naturally) and mega mochas. I picked out Better Red Than Dead, New Money Green, and extra nondairy whipped topping on my soy mocha.

It feels really good to keep my standards up.

"You're going to do so much better than Dave," Jane said as she tried on her twenty-third pair of identical black platform loafers. Easy for her to say.

"We'll find you someone to go out with. Not that you need help," Beth said as she checked out the socks.

I saw this pair of suede boarder sneakers on a display. They were the ones I helped Dave pick out a couple of weeks ago. It killed me.

Phone just rang. I ran to answer it, but first checked the Caller ID. There was Dave's parents' name, same as always. I reached for the phone. Then I stopped, wondering if I should answer it. Then it stopped ringing. I waited to see if he'd leave a message. He didn't. Then I thought since he'd probably already moved, maybe it was *his* mom calling *my* mom. Not very likely, but still. They could be commiserating. No, definitely Dave, home to get more of his stuff or a free meal, I told myself.

Plus I told myself to quit standing in the hallway by the phone having private conversations with myself about who's calling from now on.

I picked up the phone to call Dave back and tell him to quit calling and not leaving a message. But I wouldn't give him the satisfaction.

Then as soon as I put it back, the phone rang again. Mom grabbed it in the kitchen. I could hear her yelling, "What are you trying to sell?" and "How did you get this number?" and "Please take me off your call list!"

So much negative energy here, or at least phone calls. I think I'll drive up I-70 to the buffalo overlook. Gazing at the herd always makes me feel better. They're so incredibly huge, and majestic, they always make my problems seem really small. They suffered for so many years—well, not those particular ones, but their people. Their buffalo. Whatever. Slaughtered. By the thousands.

And now they have this huge piece of land that's theirs and they don't have to do anything except try to have baby buffaloes. Buffets and Buffettes.

There are better places to see buffalo, like the zoo, and buffalo ranches, where you can see them up close. But at the zoo they're fenced in and look depressed, and at ranches they're waiting to become steaks and burgers.

What's so unbelievable to me now is that the first time Dave and I went out, he ordered a buffalo burger and I asked him to change his order, and he *did*. And he asked a billion questions about why I don't eat meat, and I told him why not buffalo, and how ordering cheese on top just compounds the problem, how our whole meat-eating culture is basically wrong, we use way too much water—he didn't even fall asleep or take off for the bathroom. He just listened. And he also said I should use all that stuff on my college entrance essays.

But then we got to know each other better, and I admitted I slipped up sometimes—I actually felt close enough to him that I could admit that I liked Taco Bell. I told him it was okay for him to order whatever he wanted, that I had no right to preach when I was still sneaking ice cream at work now and then. But he still wouldn't.

Everybody else gets sick of me watching *National Geographic* and *Wild Discovery* over and over. "Not the polar bears again," Bryan's always complaining. "You've seen this like thirteen times!" Beth yells.

But Dave understood. He wouldn't watch them with me, but he understood. Sort of. I thought so, anyway.

He's a Buffalo now. I mean, he's a CU Buff. Not sure if he deserves to be.

8/28 3:42 A.M.

Just woke up from really horrible dream about Dave.
Have to write it down before I forget it.

    Damn. Forgot it already while I was writing that.

Mom is wacko. More than before.

She announced at dinner that we're all going to this big family Thanksgiving reunion at Grandma and Grandpa Callahan's in Nebraska. She's planning it three months ahead of time because the whole Von Dragen side of our clan will be there. Also because she lives for planning, right next to cleanliness and budgetliness. Like I want to see the Von Dragens after they gave me obnoxious middle initials that I have to leave off forms unless I want to be rejected from college due to my infectious nature. Repulsive middle name, boring last name. Smith.

Why can't I have a cool last name like Jane? Nakamura. Courtney Nakamura. Okay, so it doesn't really match, and I'm not Japanese, but so what?

You can't fit Von Dragen on a form. I've tried. The closest you can get is "Von Drag," and that is definitely not the impression I want to give. It's been my mission in life to keep anyone from finding out my middle name. I think the only person who knows it is Beth. Well, Beth and Dave. Of course he's already forgotten it, like he's forgotten me and my phone number.

"I thought we arranged this," I said to Mom. "I want to stay here for Thanksgiving. There's the football game, and the parade, and the *fun*." Besides, Dave might come home for a few days. It might turn out that we both grew enough in 3 months that we're ready to get back together. You know, like that fast-grow fertilizer Mom uses on the lawn. Not that it works for *her*, but that's because she buys the no-name brand left over from last year.

I shouldn't be so harsh about Mom. She really only does all this because she's a single mom now, and the three of us probably are expensive to keep up. But come on, where's all that child-support money from Dad going?

Back to reuniting with Dave. I know I've changed in the past month. For instance, I'm about a hundred times more better—oops, meant to write "bitter."

"But Courtney, your grandmother will be so hurt if you don't go," Mom said, as the phone started ringing. The phone rang like six times while we were trying to eat, and each time it was a telemarketer. Mom gets really mad. I tell her to unplug the phone, but she's made it this personal mission to yell at each and every telemarketer.

"Mom, we got Caller ID so you don't have to take those calls," I said.

"If they can disturb me? I can disturb them," she said. But the problem is she gets in this really nasty mood and all of a sudden normal topics become battles.

"Courtney, you're going, and that's final. We all have to be together," she said. "It means a lot to me. Don't you care how I feel?"

Then Bryan starts talking about how if I don't have to go, he can stay home with me—

"Okay, okay, I'll go," I said. I don't eat turkey, but does she care about that? About how it makes *me* feel—nauseous? Thanksgiving is like poultry worship. I'm not into that.

Besides, baby-sit Bryan all weekend? No thanks. I'd rather get salmonella poisoning, which is very possible at Grandpa's. He likes a moist bird—i.e., still breathing.

The only positive thing I can say about my little brother is that he has a crush on Beth. That is his *only* saving grace. Other than that, his personality is as distinctive as the dozens of crumpled tube socks scattered on his bedroom floor. "You don't get it," is his favorite expression. "I have to live with three women and no guys. Nobody gets it."

No, we don't. And we don't want to.

Deep Late-Night Reflection (a/k/a Insomnia):

Maybe this thing with Dave bothers me so much because of Dad. How he took off to be "free," but now he's married again. (Speaking of jerks.)

Then again he and Mom are happier apart; they used to fight a lot. About money, about her working as a temp accountant instead of having her own business, about the rock garden and lawn care, about everything. So him leaving and the divorce wasn't an all-bad thing, except at the time.

I wonder if Mom ever thinks about getting remarried. Of course she'd actually have to date someone first, and she hasn't done that in a long time. I told her once that she should hook up with this guy from her book club, and she told me she was against hooking up on principle. I think she thought I was talking about drugs.

Anyway, if I don't date this year and Mom doesn't . . . does that mean I'm turning into her?

Let's see. Do I wear panty hose until they're so sheer they're transparent and held together by 8 swabs of clear nail polish? No.

Do I wash out plastic bread bags and reuse them, even when they've had tuna-onion salad sandwiches in them and make peaches taste like dead skunks? No.

Do I sit with my three best friends every Saturday

morning and gossip and drink too much cheap coffee?
No. Well, sometimes. But I only have two friends.

I'll have to check this list from time to time—make
sure I don't slip into Momdom.

Dreamt I was driving to Nebraska. I was going too slowly and horses pulling covered wagons kept passing me. This little girl with a white bonnet stuck out her tongue at me as her pa's wagon dusted me. Pioneer road rage.

Then a buffalo came out of nowhere and ran out right in front of the car. I swerved so I wouldn't hit it. Only I swerved the wrong way and plowed right into the buffalo. And all the wagon people started shaking their fists at me, like I was the one responsible for slaughtering all the Plains bison.

The movie could be: *Buff Meets Bull* (our car or at least the one I'm allowed to drive is an old maroon Taurus, so I decided to go astrological and call it what it is) (anyway, I love hoofed animals, just not eating them).

Buff was now roadkill.

Bull was now totaled.

Then Jaws of Life approached to pull me from the wreckage (the pioneer wagons took off for Kansas), and I discovered Dave was sitting in the backseat.

"You could have missed her," he said. "If you just hit the brakes a little quicker." *Her!* Did he have to call the buffalo a her? Why did he care more about what happened to her than to me?

This dream was the pits. I was jealous of a BUFFALO.

We argued about my driving until I started feeling

31

really guilty: the car was totaled, a buffalo was dead . . . and Dave hated me. Then the gigantic metal Jaws of Life dropped me onto the pavement, rejecting me like a too-small fish. It was awful.

Today's Truth or Dairy trivia question:

"Who holds the record for being the most annoying person ever?" (Actually it was something about the number of Coloradans who've won Olympic medals— nobody got it.)

There is nothing worse than a failed, frustrated guidance counselor who ended up starting a business making ice cream and smoothies instead of counseling, because there was more "potential" in it. Gerry's favorite word. "Potential." I'd potentially like to whack him with the ice-cream scoop every time he says it.

We never knew him when he was a counselor at Bugling Elk—I don't think he lasted more than a year or two, tops. But it seems like he always has kids from BE working at T or D—he keeps getting people referred to him, and so he never has to work hard at hiring. It was Beth's idea we go work there. On days like today, I do so want to remind her of that. When she quit smoking, she decided a job here would be a "healthy outlet" for her. Me, I just needed some CASH. (Jane won't do it because she won't work in fast food because she's against uniforms on principle because of bad fashion. We told her it's not fast food and it's not a uni, it's an apron. She still won't even consider it.)

But anyway, the thing about Gerry is that it also seems like he never really quit counseling. It's in his blood or something.

Today at work, he said, "Courtney, I have an observation. Would you like to hear it?"

I restrained myself. I need this job. Plus it's fun, working with Beth. "Sure, Gerry!"

"I couldn't help noticing that over the past few days . . . well, don't take this the wrong way. But you're not making the sundaes and smoothies with your usual flair."

Flair? Like I'd won awards or something.

Then Gerry leaned in with his patented look of concern. "Is everything all right?" he asked me.

I had just made three Banana Splitsvilles in a row. They were works of art, as far as I was concerned. You have to stick flags with toothpicks through banana wheels and then into each scoop of ice cream, and arrange coconut and chocolate flakes in perfect symmetry with chopped pecans and walnuts, and then there's the whipped cream. I mean, it could take some people three or four minutes. I've got it down to two and a half.

"Everything's fine," I said.

"Really." He gazed into my eyes as if he were about to tell my fortune. "Everything's fine at home."

I nodded.

"At school," he said.

I nodded again.

"With Dave."

I tried to nod, but my neck got stuck in this cramp all of a sudden, and I couldn't get it to move. So instead I smiled, showing him all my teeth.

"You've been snacking on the pecans again," he said.

Busted.

I did see Grant on the way home from work, out in the parking lot. Avoided him. He'd only try to tell me something about Dave. I'm not ready.

Besides, any of Dave's friends are former friends of mine—i.e., enemies.

Oscar got a new prescription today. He looked like the world's most pathetic mutt when I got home from school. He was fritzing out—his tongue was hanging out (more than usual) and his legs were twitching and there was this trail of frothy drool around his bed. Another grand mal seizure. I hate when Oscar has seizures, it really scares me.

I called Mom at work. She said to call Dr. Wolper right away. It's cool because Dr. Wolper makes house calls and you never have to wait that long, unless she's in the middle of a surgery. She came right over when I told her about Oscar's latest seizure.

"I see this in a lot of patients like Oscar," she said as she pressed the stethoscope to Oscar's chest. "Probably needs to have his dose upped a little."

How she can find a heartbeat through all that gray fur is a mystery to me.

The funniest thing about Oscar's prescription bottle of phenobarbital is the sticker warning him not to drive after taking the medication.

"He's a dog," I told the lady at Walgreens when I went to pick up the new 'scrip.

"Then he really shouldn't be driving, should he?" she replied. Not even cracking a smile.

"Actually, he's fine during the day. He just shouldn't drive at night," I said.

I heard someone behind me laughing. So I turned

around and saw Grant "Lake" Superior standing behind me in line for a prescription. Why? I feel like I keep seeing him everywhere. His face turned red when our eyes met. Don't look at what he's picking up, I told myself. Just in case it's condoms or something private.

Who gets prescription condoms, though? I mean, that would be pretty weird.

"Um, hi," I said, stepping aside to make room for him.

"Hey." He signed the form, and the pharmacist handed him a little bag.

Grant doesn't think he's superior to anyone—you know, casting against type and all that. I remember when he used to be this really scrawny guy, the kind everyone pushes around in the lunch line back when that stuff was funny. Then last year he got taller and wider and turned into a hotty. And he still has the scrawny-guy personality, so he's like this perfect hybrid, something nature designed over time like the way certain snake species look like leaves so they can be camouflaged under a pile of leaves and then kill anything that comes close.

Not that Grant's a killer. Or a snake. In fact, if Beth were smart she would have held on to him after their little tryst last year. (Is tryst the right word? Or do I mean rendezvous?) Except for *that* disaster (remember how hurt he looked when she blew him off that day at lunch? He thought they were a couple—she was already checking out someone else), I can't think of anyone he's gone out with.

"So, um, this isn't for me," I said, pointing at the bag.

I didn't want rumors floating around that I was dumped because of some . . . infection or something. When your middle initials are V.D., you can't be too careful. "My dog has seizures unless he takes this stuff."

"Really? How come?"

"He has this head-trauma-induced epilepsy thing condition. I think that's the official term. Ever hear of it?"

"Sort of," he said.

"Basically, he got hit by a car, and it sort of scrambled his brain. For instance, sometimes he forgets where he is and he gets freaked out really easily and then he runs away and can't find his way home."

We exchanged awkward nods. I was talking too much but for some reason couldn't stop. I was about to ask him if he'd heard from Dave when he made a bolt for the door.

"Sorry about your dog. Well, gotta go," he said. "Hope . . ."

"Oscar," I said.

"Hope Oscar feels better." Then he tapped me with the crinkly white bag on his way out—on the arm, kind of intimate-like. He wouldn't do that if there was something really gross in the bag. Would he? Outside I saw him getting into this car in the blue zone—for the disabled. And he was driving it! Here I thought Grant was a nice guy. Instead he's picking up prescription condoms and parking illegally.

When I got home, after stopping at Safeway for a gigantic box of cheap hot dogs for him, Oscar was missing. Typical. I run around getting his new drugs and hot dogs to put them in, and he can't even wait for me? Bryan and I found him at the park about half an hour later. He was pawing through a trash can, and he had a bunch of spaghetti in his mouth. He does this so we look like bad owners, I swear. He's into pasta. Maybe we should put his pills in manicotti.

When we cornered Oscar and got a leash attached to his collar, this guy with a billion plastic grocery bags hanging all around his belt came up to us. He had a big button on his fishing vest that said, "Leash Be Friends." He told us we shouldn't let Oscar off his leash and that people not respecting the leash law led to death and destruction blah blah blah.

"Did you know that unleashed dogs are responsible for all of the goat killings in the Denver area?" he asked.

He was so crazy! We ran away before he leashed *us*.

When we got home we told Mom about it. She said that some goats had been brought in to control weeds in the city parks, something about a natural alternative to pesticides. So they spent the summer eating a bunch of noxious weeds and then got offed by some vicious dogs. Nice. Excellent plan. So much for natural.

Next year I bet they use those crop duster planes and just spray the hell out of the parks.

When I walk down the hallway, everyone looks at me like I have the plague. Just because I'm no longer half of a couple! As if there's a problem with that, as if it's not my ultimate *goal* right now.

I hate when people have an attitude about me. Like they've worked on it, like it matters to them. And I've never even spoken to them.

Sometimes I wish I went to an alternative school, in another country. One where there were only hardened criminals and nobody spoke to each other except in some language I couldn't understand.

Maybe everyone's looking at me weird because Grant told them about seeing me at Walgreens. Saying a prescription is for your dog is probably a really common excuse. I should have been more original. There's probably a rumor going around that I have seizures, or else there's one that I'm addicted to phenobarbital or something worse, and that's why Dave dumped me. Which would make him *so* much less of a person. If that's possible.

I can't believe he hasn't called yet. So I told him not to, he has to know that wasn't what I meant. I hate when people say they'll do something, and they don't.

I should have broken up with him first. I wanted to, you know. It crossed my mind several times. But I'm a bigger person than that, I don't break up with someone over petty things like moving to another town or living separate lives. I'm a middle child, I'm used to making sacrifices just to make things work out. But not Dave. He has to be free. And clear.

I hope he gets a really big zit on the first day of classes, from all the stress.

He won't even be able to handle college classes. And the sad thing is, he doesn't realize that.

Everywhere I go, there's this chorus of "You and Dave were such a good couple!" and "I can't believe he wants to see other people when he had you!"

I know they *mean* well.

No, actually, maybe they don't. But some of them do. I think.

In gym class today Ms. Ramstein announced that we were going to learn Tae-Bo. Jane gave me this look, like, "She can't be serious." First of all Ms. Ramstein has no idea what it is, second of all she's like a year behind the times, third of all she teaches gym but we don't know why, because she can't lift her leg higher than a foot off the floor—in any event. When she tried to teach gymnastics sophomore year, she ran into the vault at least eight times a day.

Anyway, so she's all excited because she got a video on sale at Target. "Girls, we're going to kick butt today!" she cried. Her purple cotton sweatshirt and gray sweatpants hanging off her like a 70s soft rock tune.

It was so obvious she'd only watched the video once, and maybe in slow motion. She kept calling it Tai Chi by mistake and getting all meditative, not understanding that the point of this was to kick things. With force.

"Ms. Ramstein? I think we're supposed to be like . . . madder. Or something," I finally said.

"Take a deep breath," she kept telling us. "Let it go. Let it all . . . go."

So ridiculous. Let it go. Beth's always saying that, part of her psychobabble. Where's "it" going to go? You can't expect bad things to fall off like old skin or run away once you "let go" of the leash (Oscar, anyone?). You have to push them off. That's all I was thinking. That and how much I hated Dave for ruining my senior year. How I had to forget about him or I was never going to have fun. How I needed something else, like Tae-Bo, to focus on, because I was sounding shallow even to myself.

"Ha! Ha! Ha!" I chanted with each kick.

I was so into it I didn't even notice that Jane was waving her hands in front of me to get my attention. I thought she was just personalizing the workout for herself, doing her own moves.

"Hold on, girls—I think Courtney's got the hang of it. Everyone stop and watch Courtney!"

"You've got to punch him out!" I told Ms. Ramstein. Oops. "I mean, punch it out. Your, um, anger," I said. "I mean, to get the full aerobic benefit." The music suddenly went off. I stopped kicking and started panting, totally out of breath.

When I looked up I saw this entire line of guys standing there staring at me. They had just jogged into the gym from outside.

"Hey, Courtney!" the Tom yelled from across the gym. "Nice moves!"

The other guys were all grinning, like something I did or said was funny. Which might be nice if I weren't exercising and doing Ms. Ramstein's job for her and demonstrating the stupid moves. Or what I thought were the moves, anyway. Like I know.

"What's the matter, haven't you ever seen someone do Tae-Bo before?" I yelled back.

"Yeah—and that wasn't it!" someone yelled back.

"Ignore them," Jane said. She hadn't even broken a sweat.

I'll never get a date now. Not that I want one with any of *them*.

Ms. Ramstein stopped me after class. She was squeezing sweat out of her red-white-and-blue headband. "You're a bit young to be so jaded, Courtney."

I hate when adults come up with these adjectives for me. As if they know more about me than I do. Like they *could*.

Here are my adjectives for Ms. Ramstein:

sloppy

no fashion sense

bad dresser

also, not very limber

Jane and Beth dragged me out tonight. I hate when people ambush me into going out.

"It's Friday night and we're going to have *fun*," Jane declared when she picked up me and Beth from Truth or Dairy. She had these new green glasses on, the latest from her Glasses of the Month club for extremely hip people; they get a new pair every month for a reduced price as long as they stay hip enough to sort of advertise for the place. It goes along with her haircut contract; Jane's got more contracts than the jocks at school. And better, glossier hair. She has some shoe deal, too. Must be nice.

"We're going to a concert at Juiced and Java'ed," she said. I just have one problem with that place—it's a total ripoff of T or D!!!

Except they substitute coffee for ice cream. And they book good bands and you can smoke in this tiny section and drink all the coffee you want. Which is why the line to the bathroom is always at least five people long.

"I don't know," I said. "Do we have to go out? Couldn't we just stay home and turn up our stereo really, really loud?"

Beth punched my arm. "Shut up. You know how much I love concerts. You're not going to deprive me."

That's when I remembered. My dream—I **mean**, nightmare—from a week or so ago. In it, I was at a concert. The formal kind, like the ones Alison gives with her chamber orchestra. I was all happy because I was there, sitting next to Dave. But then I realized I was there by myself—and he was there with *Beth*!!!

Also it was a really bad concert. Sting wearing a tux and playing with a full orchestra.

I can't believe Beth would steal Dave, even if it's only in my subconscious. Is it in hers? You know how sometimes your dreams tell you something you're trying not to know in real life?

I stared at her all night. Watched her every move. She seemed to be flirting with a dozen other guys that weren't named Dave, but maybe I just *wanted* to see that. We meet lots of guys when we go out, because Jane's so beautiful.

"What's wrong with you? Why do you keep looking at me instead of the band?" Beth finally asked.

"Oh. No reason." I smiled at her. "I was just afraid that you might want to smoke." *And go out with my ex-boyfriend.* "Being around all these smokers."

She shook her head. "I have so much else to live for, you know?"

Like stealing my ex-boyfriend.

"There's no way I'm ever going back to smoking." She and Jane clinked their glass mugs and drank more decaf. I started looking at the dessert menu. It was really hard to avoid the chocolate eclairs that kept going by on trays.

Got home and the Caller ID was flashing. I thought it might be Dave, but all it said for the caller's name was UNAVAILABLE. Yeah, no kidding, I wanted to say. It started with 440, which is Boulder, so I know it was Dave. (Hey, I've read *Nancy Drew*, okay? Or actually I think what I read was Sue Grafton, Mom keeps buying used copies at yard sales.)

But Dave didn't leave a message. What kind of call is that? He wants me to know he's thinking of me, but he doesn't want to actually talk to me or have me call him back?

I actually slept with him. Like, more than once.

Why? When he's going to be such a jerk, leaving no messages and sleeping with my best friend?

Actually I didn't sleep with him that many times. Maybe that's why he dumped me. Well, too bad. He *said* it was okay, that we had plenty of time for that in the future.

What a liar!

I called Beth. "I just wanted to make sure you got home okay," I said when she answered.

"Courtney. Jane dropped me off first," Beth said. "You saw me walk into my house!"

"Yeah. I know. I'm just sort of . . . paranoid lately," I said. "So, did you get any phone calls while you were out?"

"A couple," she said. "Nothing good. Just this guy named Rand who I met at work last week, I thought he was cute so I gave him my number, but then I realized I can't go out with someone named *Rand*. And this other guy, Bill? Remember me talking about him?"

Beth doesn't have a "little black book" for all the guys she goes out with occasionally. She practically has a zip drive.

Which only makes me more suspicious.

I just looked over the last 3 entries. Every other sentence starts with "I hate when."

I have to stop hating so incessantly. I need to be more positive, or no one will want to be around me. Like last night when I kept saying how I hated when other people cut in front in line, and I hated when there was no toilet paper in the bathroom stall and nobody reported it, and I hated when bands played for only 45 minutes after I waited 2 hours in line to buy the tickets to see them—

Well, anyway. You get the point. I get the point. I can't Tae-Bo my way through life. It's a great workout, but a little hostile.

And that stuff about Beth going out with Dave? That would never happen. Paranoid, jealous, hateful. I resolve not to go through life like that. Beth would never go out with Dave; she doesn't like being more than 10 seconds away from the guys she's seeing, for one thing. For another, he's so annoying—and she isn't. I love Beth. I trust Beth.

And I want to embrace life. Not kick its ass.

I hate when I'm self-critical. Like in what I wrote yesterday. So what if I hate things? I can't like everything. Not even close.

So I might as well not hate myself, right?

And Beth is acting suspicious. She hasn't made a move on anyone in the past month that I know about. Which must mean *something*.

Okay, so I sort of formalized this pledge today and I guess I should write it in here. It's going to sound so predictable when I write it down because it's something I've believed for a really long time.

So here it comes: I am not going to get involved with anyone my senior year. No guys. No girls, either. Don't get me wrong. I'm not giving up on guys *completely*. I just don't want to get involved with anyone senior year because we'll have to break up at the end of the year, apparently that's the way it's done and I was a fool not to realize it earlier.

"Just do what I do! Don't get serious with anyone," Beth said.

"But I don't work like that," I told her. "I'm a very serious person."

"You're serious," she said. "About being serious?"

"How can you doubt me so much?" I asked her. It's okay for me to doubt her. She's the one showing up in my dreams.

So once I made this decision, I had to tell Jane, too. We were sitting in French class. Jane actually looked *un peu* French with her new glasses and haircut. I scribbled her my decision and asked her to sign the piece of paper, as a witness. She signed it and wrote, "This is so perfect!"

"*En français*," I wrote back, as a joke. But then I realized what she'd just said. My life being ruined for an entire year, sitting home alone, night after night, was "perfect"?

"Were you jealous of me being with Dave or something?" I asked her after class.

Jane was so excited about her idea, she didn't even hear me. "If you are absolutely sure you're not going out with *anyone* this year, it means *you* can run for vice president! You can make our senior year great."

There's this sudden vacancy in the student council spot because the vice prez, Jennifer Scher, used to go out with the prez, Tom Delaney, last year before they were elected. The Tom is very good-looking and has gone out with at least half the girls in this school. Including Beth, naturally. He has this irresistible quality, according to Beth, you don't know when it's going to hit you but it does. He's the kind of guy who uses flowers and jewelry as weapons, if you know what I mean. He also dresses really well, like, all the time. He wears all this Tommy Hilfiger stuff as if he's the Tommy who designed it.

Anyway, it looked like he had sort of settled down with Jennifer, they went out for like 6 months. Then as soon as they started student council this year, Tom had a fling with the secretary and totally upset Jennifer. Does he quit? Resign? No. He makes Jennifer's life so miserable that *she* does.

Just like a guy. Just like a president.

So all of a sudden our class projects are going nowhere, because Jennifer was like the driving force behind everything.

"Okay. I'll think about it," I told Jane. It's not like I have anything else to do with my time. Besides, being on student council would look good for my law school applications.

What am I going to do next year, anyway? Go to college, duh. But where? Should I try to go where Alison went, make it a Smith Family Tradition? The Stafford brochure said something about "producing great men and women for over a century." Like it's a factory, like we're shoes.

My wish list for the future:
go to a good school
make sure Dave is not at that school
make sure Beth and Jane are within driving distance
unless it's an incredibly long drive
then I'll fly
get into law school—Ivy League
sue Dave for emotional distress
become a righteous prosecutor in tradition of Marcia Clark, only win cases
then go on to become CNN commentator like her
but with better makeovers

Talked with Grant after Life Issues today. We spent half an hour learning ways of coping with change and making lists to help us cope. It all boiled down to the fact that you basically just have to change, you won't like it, and you can forget about coping with it. Anyway, after spending all that time listening to people talk about their big life changes (switching cell phone companies, dealing with new hairstyles, etc.), I was suddenly desperate for that info on Dave that Grant kept trying to tell me. I had to know if he's as miserable as I am. But at first Grant just said he had a "great" roommate and really liked his "great" dorm and his classes were all "great."

Excuse me, but that's a little too perfect. It has to mean Dave's lying. He probably *told* Grant to say all that stuff.

So then Grant asked how I was doing. I started telling him. I wanted to give him a perfect story for Dave. About how fabulously I was doing, about how I had a fabulous new boyfriend and had actually been recruited by three fabulous colleges. All of them in Boston—no, Europe.

But the next thing I knew I was pouring out my guts to Grant, telling him gruesome details that no boy should know, like about how I couldn't sleep at night and how I had started watching 90210 reruns instead of nature shows, and right now the only ones on were from back when David was nerdy and short and Kelly slept around.

53

"God, why am I telling you all this? I'm sorry," I finally said. "I should go."

"No, don't," Grant said. "I mean, it's okay. I understand."

"You do?" Somehow I doubted that. Had he gone out with Dave for a year? And if he had, did I want to know that?

"Sure. I haven't been there, but it has to be really hard, breaking up with someone after so long. I bet, actually, that it really sucks," he said.

For some reason that made me laugh. "Yeah. It does. But I guess it's not the end of the world or anything."

"So . . . have you guys talked to each other at all?" Grant asked. "Since then?"

"No. He said he'd call," I told him. "And he does call. But he doesn't leave messages. And he always calls when he knows I'm not home."

"I don't know, that's probably just a coincidence. Why don't you call him?" Grant asked.

"Because he said *he'd* call. And the one who gets broken up with can't call the breaker upper," I explained.

"Oh." He nodded. "I guess you're right."

"He said we were meant for each other. What did he *mean* by that? People don't just say things like that and not mean them."

Grant's face turned sort of red. "Well . . . yeah, Courtney. They do. A lot of guys do, anyway."

"They do?" It was like I was doing an interview with a scientist about another species. Tonight on *Wild*

Discovery: Males.

That's it. I'm through with boys. Until college, and that'll be far from here. I'll show *him* long-distance. "So when they say something serious to you . . . they really don't mean it. At all."

He looked very thoughtful for a few seconds. "Some of them do. I do. Anyway, it's not just guys that lie. Girls do, too—a lot of the time."

All of a sudden I got this very clear idea he was thinking about Beth when he said that. Like when they were making out and dancing that night, he'd said he really liked her, and he meant it. And she didn't. I was kind of shocked that it still bothered him.

"Yeah." I cleared my throat. I was kind of uncomfortable about this conversation going any further, because then I'd have to defend Beth, and I didn't necessarily know if I could. "Well, I didn't mean to um . . . say that all guys were evil—"

"And I didn't mean to say anything about—"

"It's okay," I interrupted him. "So, um, see you around."

"Right. Sure," Grant said. "And don't worry about Dave, because, you know, you're going to be okay."

"I'll just use some of my new *coping* skills," I told him.

Grant laughed, and I noticed he has this chip out of his front tooth. Either it's from ice hockey or it's from the getting-pummeled years. That's one thing I really like about him, you never know. "Go home tonight and make some lists," he said. "I'm sure you'll feel a lot better."

So here's my list based on the brilliant concept that "change is inevitable." (Hold on, I thought that was "death.")

Mr. Antero told us to ask ourselves: What can I do to deal with this inevitable change?

1. Hate Dave.

2. Try to move on by getting involved with other things. Which I am already doing by joining student council.

3. Stop obsessing about Dave. Which I will do this instant.

The Tom endorsed me today.

No, that's not new lingo for "hit on me," although with the Tom you really never know.

He literally endorsed me, for vice president of the student council. Like, he put up these signs and posters advertising me as Tom Delaney's Choice.

Then again, I don't know why I'm surprised. I mean, of course he's going to endorse me, I'm a *girl*, and I'm the only girl running for the office, and I'm a girl he hasn't scored with yet. Big challenge there, winning him over.

But he's actually trying to be nice or something. He cornered me at lunch and said how I'm the best person for the job, and how I shouldn't listen to anything negative Jennifer says—if I get the job, I should take it.

Naturally I went and found Jennifer right away.

"I don't want to talk about *him*," Jennifer said. "I'm moving on with my life." She was cleaning out her locker at the time. Perhaps that should have given me a clue.

I begged her for details, so I'd know what to be prepared for. I told her I knew what it was like to have your heart broken, that I was going through the same thing.

But before we could really bond, her parents walked up and said, "Ready to go, then?"

Turns out she's transferring to another school—a private one, in another state. That's how much she hates the Tom. She started walking away, but then she stopped and came back to me.

"There are things you really need to know about him," she said.

"Like never to say yes when he offers me a back rub?" I asked. (Beth told me that was Move 1.)

"Yeah. But it goes way beyond that," Jennifer said. "You have to really watch him, keep track of everything he does—"

"Jennifer? Come on, we're double-parked," her mother said. "And talking about that boy is just a waste of your time." She pulled Jennifer away.

"Thanks!" I called. "For the warning!"

Like I needed one.

I wrote Alison an e-mail and thought it was so good I'd print it and paste it in here instead of writing:

Dear Alison,

Sure, you can laugh. You're living it up, going to frat parties every night. Me, I'm stuck here, bored out of my skull. When exactly am I coming for my prospective student visit? Let's make it October. No, wait—how about tomorrow?

Mom won't even notice I'm gone. She's too busy planning our Thanksgiving family reunion wagon train to Nebraska. *Already.* She told me you decided to go to a friend's house nearby instead of making the trek to the Von Dragens of Ogallala. How could you do that to me? Mom told me I'm in charge of "all the breads" for the meal. What does *that* mean?

If that isn't enough to make me crazy, then how about sharing a car with Mom, Bryan, and Oscar for 4 hours? Don't you love me anymore?

Courtney

The frat party thing was a joke. Alison's not really the kegger type. She has a bunch of friends from the music department, and they sit around practicing together. It would be annoying if she weren't so good. But then her being so good is annoying, too, in its own way. "Don't you have an instrument, Courtney?" all the teachers would ask when I came into their classes. After a while I just started holding up my pen.

Oops—she wrote back already! Here's her reply.

Dear Courtney,
You didn't mention anything about Dave. What's going on?
Are you okay? Have you heard from him?
Love, Alison

Dear Alison,
No! God, no. Do you think that's my whole life or something? Dave?

Wonder what Dave's new e-mail address is. I wonder
if I could find him on Yahoo?

"Phase three," Beth told me when I was reminiscing
about Dave at work today. "Acceptance."

"Phase four," I said. "You quit observing my phases. I
feel like the moon."

"Interesting metaphor, Courtney." Gerry nodded.
"You feel like the moon. You see yourself as a celestial
body. Out there in your own private world, in outer
space."

"She could be feeling independent," Beth said. "That
would be good. Because she broke the chain, she com-
pleted the cycle."

Excuse me while I go into the ladies' room and get my
period. All this stupid talk about moons and cycles. It
sort of made me want to forget about being a lawyer and
sign up for the NASA shuttle. Just to get away from the
psychological profiles.

Talk about having a bad weekend. I disgust myself sometimes.

I was giving Oscar his pill tonight—phenobarbital in a budget value hot dog, delish—and all of a sudden I wanted a hot dog.

I cooked 2 in the toaster oven and ate them right away.

I melted *cheese* on top of them. Not even good cheese, but those watery American slices Mom buys in 5 pound blocks. Then I put on ketchup, mustard, relish, and even some Frank's Hot Sauce.

I feel so gross now. I should have eaten Oscar's pills instead of his hot dogs. They're not even good hot dogs, they're the kind you buy 40 at a time because they're for a dog. Dogs for a dog. I wish I was one of those people who could make herself throw up.

I called Beth and told her I'd slipped up. "You mean, you broke your dumb no-dating law? You went *out* with someone?" She sounded really excited.

"No, of course not," I said. "I ate a hot dog. Okay, two."

"Ewww," she said. "Courtney, are you all right? Do you want me to come over? You know, that reminds me of the time that I was really upset about not getting into the arts school and I chain-smoked all night. Which wasn't that long after you didn't get the summer internship at that law firm and I took you out for dinner and you had a big fat steak and a crème brulée—remember?"

At this rate we might as well have eating disorders, except we lack the discipline. Maybe Beth and I need to be hospitalized, though. We should be. Maybe instead of going to college. Could save a lot of money on red meat, fat, and cigarettes.

"Courtney Smith. *You're* running?"

Suzanne Stupemeier stopped me in the hallway this morning.

I hate when people my age talk to me like that. It's like, get out of your minivan, take off your soccer-mom sunglasses and your cardigan sweater, put down your Tupperware container and just *talk* to me.

This student council vice-president thing wasn't my idea, okay? My friends made me do it because I'm the only one who can stand up to the Tom's hormones, or hormone, actually—testosterone. The one element I can remember from Health Issues, the junior year class to teach you things you don't learn in school but that you take at school.

And I wasn't sure I was *going* to do it until I had a precollege-application meeting with my guidance counselor yesterday and she pointed out although my grades were excellent, except for that incident in Driver's Ed, the extracurricular section of my college apps was a little blank.

"You might want to add a few things here," she said. "They like . . . active applicants."

Sexually active? I thought. Really? Because right now I don't have a shot in hell—

Mrs. Greene must have seen me blushing. "You know, well-rounded people, who get involved at school, play sports, and have interests outside of school."

"Oh. Right." I sighed. That kind of active. "Well, I do have a job," I said.

"Yes." Mrs. Greene nodded. "You do have that." She made it sound like a disease. What's so bad about working at Truth or Dairy?

"And I adopted that highway," I reminded her.

"You and a group of a hundred others," Mrs. Greene reminded *me*.

When it came to sports, I had nothing to say. I was just sort of average at everything. But hey, not everyone can be on varsity teams. Especially not Jane, because she hates uniforms, though we talked about it once and both agreed it would be cool to have a number.

Okay, back to my campaign.

"Well, what *are* your ideas?" Suzanne asked me.

"I'm working on my platform," I said. Does anyone in student council do anything but organize parties anyway? Is it that important?

"I heard you were antigay. Is that true?" She picked a pill off her sweater. "Because that's really wrong. I guess."

"Not anti*gay*, anti*guy*," I said.

That sort of stumped her. "Well, how do you differ from your opponents?"

"Uh . . . they're all guys?" I said. Because Tom's gone out with too many girls and been too mean to them for any other girl to run. Talk about a gender gap.

How he got elected in the first place, I have no idea. Maybe we were all voting for the couple, Jennifer and

Tom. They would have been prom king and queen, if they'd lasted.

"But anyway, Suzanne, I'm really devoted to the cause," I went on. "Our school's the best. We need to leave a legacy." Of truth, justice, and the American way, I should have said next. Family values! Suzanne was a bit of a Primster.

"Exactly," she said. "And our legacy is . . . ?"

"Growing every day," I told her. Like a freaking houseplant. "Like our . . . futures." Or maybe our waistlines. Or maybe the waiting lists at the colleges we want to get into but don't have a chance at.

"Exactly!" she said. "That's exactly how I look at it, Courtney. You have my vote. But I don't have to hate guys. Or gays. Right?"

"Of course not. Freedom of choice," I said. "That's what it's all about. Being . . . you know. Free and clear."

"God." She gazed at me for a second. "You're so *smart*."

Okay, this is really bizarre. You know how I've been seeing Grant everywhere lately? A few times when I leave work, and at Walgreens, etc. Like, everywhere I turn? Mind you, it's not a bad *view*. When you get right down to it, I probably think he's the most underrated senior guy in terms of looks, but he's always hiding in these standard plaid shirts and nondescript jeans, half the time he blends into the crowd. But not today.

I got off of work and he was *right* behind me in the parking lot when I went to get my car. I felt like I was on the Monday night TV movie, *The Acquaintance Beside Her, Constantly, Dogging Her Heels*. There was *his* car. Next to mine.

"Hi, Grant." I waved, all friendly-like. (It's supposed to be the best way to throw off intruders.) He waved back. "So, um, Grant," I said, trying to be casual. I was glad to see he wasn't parking in the disabled zone anymore. "Why do you keep following me?"

He gave me this weird look. Well, sure, who wouldn't after they'd been busted. *Get over me*, I wanted to say. You talked to me—don't you know? I'm unavailable this year. For dating, for fun, for like . . . life.

"What? Oh, no. I wasn't following you, Courtney," he said. "I was—"

"Look, never mind," I said. "I'm in a hurry."

"So am I!" He made this face at me, as if I was

being a real jerk. And suddenly I realized what was going on.

"Are you keeping tabs on me or something? For Dave?" I asked.

His face got all red. "Are you serious?" he scoffed.

"Well, *are* you?" I asked.

"*No,*" he said. "You know, not everything's about you and Dave!"

Oh, how I wish that were true. "Look, Grant, you're nice and all, and I appreciate you talking to me the other day. But you can't go around following people just because your friends ask you to—it's not cool."

"You're going to tell me about cool?" He stared at my black-and-white cow apron. I was in such a hurry to get home that I'd forgotten to take it off.

"I have a job, okay?" I muttered.

"So do I," Grant said. He was about to go on when I jumped into my car and slammed the door. I know it was rude, but he was acting so weird, I had to get out of there. He was practically picking a fight with me.

Lighten up, Lake Superior. I think I'll copy my class and work schedules and put them in his locker just to make this easier for him. Like he doesn't know my work schedule already. I mean, how much shopping can one person do at the Canyon Boulevard stores? You've got your pet shop, your dry cleaner's, your pizza place, a fabric store, some tax place that's only open from January to April, and an insurance office. And Truth or Dairy.

The only original place in the bunch.

Can't believe I've been working there over a year already. Time flies when you're separating frozen banana chunks.

The Over-the-Hill-and-through-the-Woods-to-Grandma's-House Campaign continued at dinner tonight.

"We'll leave at twelve that Wednesday," Mom said. "It's a five-hour drive, so we'll get there just in time to help with the pies." She had a stack of index cards in front of her. Turkey leftover recipes she's already excited about making and storing in plastic bags.

"Mom, it's two months *away*," Bryan said. "And it's not five hours, it's four. And what's the big deal?"

"The big deal is that this is a long trip, and we need to plan ahead, and we need to factor in an extra hour in case of bad weather," Mom said. She started her lecture on the virtues of planning.

Bryan took another helping of pasta. Oscar gazed up at him with intense love in his eyes, dying to get a mouthful of rotini.

I tuned them out and started thinking about the reasons I need to stay here. Index cards, please.

1—Don't want to spend multiple hours in a car with family.

2—Hate turkey. Grandpa won't even consider free range. Grandma won't even consider me not eating everything on my plate, which will be approx. 2 lbs of turkey.

3—Don't want to spend multiple days at Grandma and Grandpa's with family.

4—Could see Dave, back in town to visit his family for weekend, could get together, share a passionate night of romance, rediscover lost love for each other—

"Courtney, you and Grandma are sharing the guest room," Mom said. "You can both sleep in the queen bed—"

"What?" I asked. Was she joking? "She and Grandpa—"

"Are not getting along that well these days," Mom said.

"They don't share the same room?" I asked.

"Oh, not for a while."

Whoa. The secrets this family is hiding. What next?

"In fact, they have what you might call an 'open' relationship," Mom said.

"What? Mom, what are you saying?" I demanded.

"Your grandmother's gone on a few dates lately. Nothing serious, but—"

"Are they getting a divorce?" Bryan asked. "They're like . . . seventy. Can't they sort of stick it out at this point?"

"They might. But they have some . . . problems. You know."

Bryan and I looked at each other. I think we both knew what she was getting at, but I shut up right then. I didn't want to know what the "you know" was referring to.

My parents are divorced . . . my grandparents are having sex problems . . . my grandparents are having affairs. . . . Doesn't *anyone* in this family know how to have a relationship?

It's good to have something else to focus on, but not something that makes me this nervous. I have to give a speech for my vice-president gig, in front of the entire school. So here goes. I'll use the rest of this page—make it short but sweet. I'll write it *now*, get it out of the way, no procrastinating.

"Hi. My name is Courtney Smith. I see a lot of familiar faces out there."

And they're all scowling at me. Laughing hysterically. I've probably got a scrap of toilet paper stuck to my shoe. And my face is as red as my hair, the way my skin gets when I'm nervous, all the blood rushing to the surface in fight-or-flight mode. But I must go on. This is for . . . history. This is for . . . my entrance applications.

I have to get in somewhere really good. Dave and I were going to both go to CU, but that plan is definitely off. The school might have over 20,000 students, but that's not enough. Besides, he'd probably think I was following him there, chasing him, refusing to believe it's over.

Like I *would*.

"Thanks for taking time to listen to me today. If elected, I will . . . ban dating between seniors and juniors. Nobody will be allowed to break up with someone on the eve of the new school year. Labor Day will become the new Valentine's Day . . . a time to show your love instead of your really rotten and mean side."

"Also, we need more vegetarian lunch choices."

No. I'm going to push the school to be even better. "We need more vegan lunch choices."

Grandma just called to see how I was doing. I thought she wanted to sympathize with me about the Dave situation. They met Dave; they know Dave; they love Dave. I hoped she wouldn't be rubbing it in, how perfect we seemed together.

Not to worry. I had just begun to tell her how much my life sucked when she launched into this long story about Grandpa and did I know how hard it was to live with a man for 50 years blah blah blah. Please don't go into details, I thought. Please don't tell me about the guy from the bingo palace you're dating now.

I rushed her off the phone but not before she got in the phrase "my needs are not being met."

Like *mine* are?

Football game tonight. Could not have been weirder.
Kept seeing all these people from last year's senior class,
and they kept asking me how Dave was. I told them I
couldn't talk because I had to get to my student council
booth.

Mrs. Martinez, the faculty advisor, thought it would
be good if the candidates mingled with the public, and
what better time than during a football game when
Bugling Elk is so busy losing by 50 points that everyone
has lots of time to chat. Everyone still goes to the games,
because it's fun anyway.

So me and three guys were hanging around this table
over by the hot dog stand. Two of them were telling
everyone that if they got elected they'd make sure
Bugling Elk hires a better coach. The other guy told
everyone he would disband the football team and put the
money into chess club competitions.

Then there was me. Saying how the important thing
about sports was to stay involved and participate, and not
every team could win—even the Broncos had bad seasons
sometimes, right?

"Courtney has a point." The Tom strolled up and
stood beside me. Then he kept telling everyone who
stopped by that I'd do a good job.

The other candidates kept glaring at me.

"You're just supporting her because she's a girl," they
accused the Tom.

"She's not a girl," the Tom said. "Not like *that*."

"Hello! I'm right here, you don't have to talk about me in the third person. And what does that mean?" I asked, poking him in the chest.

"Nothing! It's just . . . you're different. Unique!" Tom said like he'd had a brainstorm.

In that I haven't made out with you yet—yes. "So are we done campaigning?" I asked. "Can I go?" Because I'd said "hi" so many times my face was getting a cramp.

The 3 guys looked at me and shrugged. The Tom shrugged.

"Okay then, *I'm* going," I said. "And I'm still a girl."

I rushed off looking for Jane and Beth. I didn't see Jane anywhere, but I spotted Beth in the smoking area, which has a new location this year: right next to one end zone of the football field. It can't be next to the school, so it's next to the sports area. *That* makes sense. Bring on the oxygen tanks. Anyway, I could see Beth over there visiting her old smoker friends. No doubt showing them those wallet-sized photos she has of blackened lungs.

Saw Grant pull up and park in disabled spot again. I was running over to tell him how wrong that was—didn't he know there were plenty of BEHS students and parents who needed those spots?

Then he helped this older lady out of the car. She had a cane and walked unevenly, like she'd broken her hip. Oops. Must be his grandmother. Instead of being a creep, he is the type of guy who drives his grandmother to football games and picks up her prescriptions. I completely misjudged him. Or rather I'm back to my original judgment.

"Courtney?" he said.

"Oh, um hi. I was just looking to see if Jane's here yet. Have you seen a white Acura?"

"Jane's in the bleachers. She's waving at you." Grant pointed behind me.

"Oh. Okay. Well, bye!" I started to run off.

I was halfway up the bleachers when the Bulging Elk mascot grabbed me in a bear hug. (Idea: if I become VP, outlaw mascots.) He has these furry antlers, and they kept poking me in the eye.

"Get away from me!" I said.

He picked up his bullhorn and made this horrible bugling noise. I nearly lost my hearing. He bugled again, because our team was for once about to score. Then the crowd went wild, everyone was bugling and yelling and screaming so loudly that the quarterback couldn't get anyone on the team to hear him. They got a delay-of-game penalty and then there was an interception in the end zone and the other team ran it all the way back down the field and scored. Oops.

Ditched the mascot with bad timing and found Beth and Jane sitting on the top bleacher because it's the best place to scope the boys. Bryan was up there, too, with his sophomore friends. All really pimply and angry about not having driver's licenses or facial hair. No doubt they were up there because it must also be the best place to scope girls, like cheerleaders. Bryan's not really the cheerleader type. He's making it his life's mission to find someone as perfect as Beth.

When I got to the top bleacher, Beth and Bryan were laughing about something, completely violating the sophomores/seniors boundary line up there. I immediately sat in between them and then moved us over, away from Bryan. I'll never get elected if I let this sort of stuff happen.

Tonight was definitely not your normal football game. But on the plus side, I think I am finally getting over Dave. I didn't really miss him tonight. Not *much*.

Anyway, to celebrate, and also because I'm now writing on inside back cover, I'm starting my new journal tomorrow. New journal, new life. Plus I can carry it around and look cool, plus it won't have anything about Dave in it. It's been over a month since we split. That's history now. He's history.

Still can't believe this! Not that this is a fresh cool sketch-book, but *THIS*, which was waiting for me in the mail drop when I got home from work.

Dear Courtney,

Hi! How are you? I know you're probably wondering why it took me so long to write. I've been thinking about you a lot. But it seemed like we needed some time apart. I hope you're not still mad at me. I didn't mean to hurt your feelings. It just seemed like the only thing to do at the time.

How is school going? How's Beth? How's Jane? I hope you guys are having fun.

School is okay. The classes are pretty intense, especially this Intro to Geology one. I thought I knew a lot about geology, but I'm really bad at memorizing stuff. My roommate, Chad, and I get along fine. He has a monster stereo, so we're always getting in trouble for playing it too loudly. He's really into rap, so I call him Puff Chaddy.

I should probably go now. I have class in twenty minutes and it's on the other side of campus. I'm so glad I got that new bike last spring. I use it every day. Thanks for helping me pick it out. When I ride, I think a lot about our trip to Taos and how much fun it was exploring the bike trails together (after we finally ditched my parents).

I hope you're doing well. I miss you.
Dave

I'm still in too much of a state of a shock to write. Plus this new journal is sort of intimidating. Too many wide-open spaces. Tomorrow.

I know I should be sleeping, but I have been up all night analyzing Dave's letter, like at a crime lab. Boyfriend Forensics. Or I guess it would be Ex-Boyfriend Forensics.

Several lines bear repeated reading. It seems to me there are 4 important items:

(1) *Actually the first one is that he didn't mention any girls. Not a single one.*

(2) *"I've been thinking about you a lot" and "I think a lot about our trip to Taos." Clearly having remorse. Obsessing. I am constantly on his mind.*

(3) *"It just seemed like the only thing to do at the time." "At the time" implies there are other options now. Also implies he made a big mistake and realizes that now.*

(4) *"I miss you."*

I don't know how he could have made it any plainer. There's only one thing to do. He *wants* me to do this.

Does car insurance cover natural disasters? And how much does that make the premium go up when you're 17 and it already takes all your allowance plus a part-time job to pay for?

And why do these things always have to happen to me? Why? Just when everything seemed so clear, so obvious . . . so easy.

I set out for Boulder to see Dave at about 3. Didn't want to look too eager, besides, had to be in school all day. But I figured if I got there on a Friday we could patch things up and then spend the weekend together. Beth tried to talk me out of it, but then I showed her The Letter. She gave me a coupon she won for a free Big Gulp and told me to hit the road. I brought all my favorite CDs and I was blasting them on the stereo as I cruised down the highway. Everything seemed perfect. My life felt like a movie for some reason. *Thelma and Louise*. Without Brad Pitt in the backseat. And not in a cool convertible.

When I started heading west on 36, the sky had a sort of black section, over the Flatirons. It wasn't that unusual, really—typical Colorado 3:00 thunderstorm. But this one was like . . . superthunder. Extra loud. All of a sudden I heard this big boom, and it shook the highway pavement, I swear. Then hail—giant ice balls—started thwacking against the windshield. I couldn't see anything! The hail was actually the size of golf balls. I felt like each one was going to smash the glass, and I kept cringing with each one, until my shoulders were even with my ears. I was so crouched over I could barely see over the steering wheel. I was driving like my grandmother.

I pulled over at the next exit and stopped at the first gas station I saw, my heart pounding in my throat. I ran into the Complete station. (Complete station. So badly named. So *completely* lacking.)

A whole bunch of Dave's friends were in there. Grant (still following me apparently), the Tom, Pete and Paul Desaulnier, Gary Matthews. What did they do, drive a minivan?

"Courtney?" The Tom was gazing out the window. "You're supposed to park *under* something."

"Oh." I'd kind of forgotten to save the car in my panic to save myself.

"Hello, Dent Clinic," Paul joked. "Can we make an appointment for tomorrow? Yes, it's a maroon Ford Taurus with a bunch of vegetarian bumper stickers—"

"Save the Tofu? Is *that* what that says?" Pete laughed. "More like save the Taurus. For my *grand*parents."

The thing about being identical twins is that you have identically bad jokes. And it's not a Taurus, it's the Bull.

"Where are you going?" Grant asked, having the decency to seem concerned.

"Um . . . shopping," I said. "You?"

"We're going to see Dave." Tom said it like it was the most natural thing in the world. He knew it bugged me, and he smiled when he said it. Do I *want* to be on student council with this jerk? Who's so devoted to Dave that he's basically a clone?

I'd rather be outside in the raging hailstorm. It would have been less painful.

"He planned this killer weekend for us, including a big party tonight at his dorm, meeting tons of college girls, then we're going to the CU football game tomorrow, and—" Blah blah blah. If he didn't kill me by going on, I was going to grab a plastic knife off the Snack Station and start stabbing myself.

All of a sudden Grant stepped in front of Tom holding a stack of napkins from the Snack Station. Then he reached up and put his hand in my hair. I felt this shivering sensation from him standing so close. It went all the way down my back, and it was cold. "What are you . . . doing?" I asked.

He pulled a couple of ice hunks out of my hair. "Your hair's kind of . . . full of ice," he said.

I reached up and felt malted-milk-ball-size hail in my hair. It was melting hail sliding down the back of my coat that was making me shiver—not stupid Grant Superior and his CU-bound buddies.

"Excuse me," I muttered, and I ran into the bathroom. The last thing I want is for them all to go to Boulder and tell Dave how horrible I looked. So I turned on the hand dryer and bent over, sticking my head underneath, until I smelled something burning. All the blood had rushed to my face, and now I had flyaway hair. Disaster two for the day.

When I came out, the guys were still there, but the hailstorm had ended, so I rushed past them, bought a fruit juice, and waved good-bye. No, really. See ya. It's been real.

The roads were covered in icy hail, and I kept sliding all over the road, it was like driving on gumballs or jawbreakers must be. But I had to get out of there. I drove up to see the buffalo herd, to make sure they were okay. And to think about other things for a while. The hail was a couple inches deep on the ground, so I was worried when I didn't see them right off. Then I realized the buffalos were all standing on the downslope, under trees. Their brown hides looked drier and better than my matted hair. "Hi, guys!" I called. They wouldn't come over to the fence, which is cool, they hardly ever do, and their hoofs might slip on the ice anyway. But it made me sad, for some reason. Like I had nothing, and no one.

I drove home going about 5 miles an hour. There was killer rush-hour traffic. As I sat there, waiting to merge, the sun came out, and I realized the hood had dozens of dents. Large ones. The car looks like it has acne pit scars. I told Mom when I got home, but she seemed curiously unconcerned, too busy yelling at a telemarketer who was calling to offer a special deal on hail-damaged car repair. "I won't give him the satisfaction!" she seethed.

"You might," I said. "I mean, maybe you should take their number—"

"That's it!" She slammed down the phone. "Is there

no privacy in American society today? I'm ordering continuous call blocker."

"But my friends—Mom, you can't do that!" Bryan protested.

"They'll get special codes to punch in," Mom said. "Their calls will go through. But no one else's!"

I could almost see her not giving Dad the special code for a few weeks. She can be so vindictive.

Mom saw the Bull in direct sunlight. My car privileges have been revoked for the next week. Will have to ride my bike to school, work, etc., and also beg Beth for rides. As if it's my fault that a cold front raced across the foothills. The weather guy on Channel 9 didn't know it was coming—but somehow I was supposed to? "It's hard enough for me to afford two cars," she said. "And now this?"

"I'm sorry, Mom," I said, over and over. I did really feel bad about it.

Mom has zero sympathy for the fact I did it all out of love. She said I shouldn't be driving to Boulder to see Dave; he should be driving here to see *me*. He has to make the first move, she said. I pointed out the letter. She said anyone can write a letter; but it's when they show in person that you know they mean it.

She went into this long, detailed story about how one time this guy wanted her back and drove across the country to apologize and beg her to move to DC and marry him. She got this really dreamy look on her face. I thought about the pictures of Mom in college with her friends, dressed up for parties, laughing, and how pretty she was. She's still pretty, don't get me wrong. She just wears all these clothes that work against her; they're all called Princeton Harbor or Sage Garden Grove or something like that. They're her country-club-wanna-be outfits. Actually she looks good in them, I just wish she'd meet

85

some guy who was *in* the club. She could quit worrying about money and I could have a new car.

"So he drove all the way out to Ogallala from Washington—this was right after college, and I was home for the summer. And his car was full of roses," Mom went on. "It was so romantic. My parents were so shocked, my father told him he could have my hand in marriage before he even *asked*—"

"And . . . was that Dad?" I said.

"Oh, no. Heavens, no." Mom's face got all red. It's the first time I've seen her blush in a long time. "This guy was a complete phony. He said he loved me, but." She shook her head. "He didn't mean it."

I could practically hear birds singing. It was this magic moment where I realized Mom and I might actually have something in common.

Then the phone rang. I grabbed it. It was Beth, calling to ask how my visit went. She said she'd been waiting to call, that she was on pins and needles. I explained the hailstorm, the Complete disaster.

"Wow. I hate to say this, but in a way it's a relief," Beth said.

"What is?"

"Well, what happened yesterday . . . it's like a sign. It means you guys aren't meant for each other," Beth said. "If you were, the heavens wouldn't have opened and thrown golf balls at you."

"It's called a weather system," I said. "It has nothing to do with fate."

"Oh, *really*. And that's why it happened at the *exact* moment you needed the roads to be clear," Beth said. "You ran into those guys at the gas station—"

"Because we left school at the same time and traveled at the same speed," I said. "It's like an algebra word problem. It's not a *sign*."

"Just accept it, Courtney. Don't fight it," Beth said. "You have to try giving up on Dave again, and it might feel even harder this time, but it'll be easier, I promise."

"Beth? I love you to death. But don't talk to me about quitting Dave like it's quitting a really bad nicotine habit," I said. "Because cigarettes don't write letters begging you to come back."

"Is that what his letter said?" Beth asked.

I reread the letter. Maybe he didn't beg me, but he was definitely hinting at a reunion. Just . . . not that strongly, maybe. Because his phone number isn't in the letter.

I called Directory Assistance, but there's no phone in his name. "Do you have a listing for a . . . Chad?" I said. The operator laughed at me. It's not a sound you want to hear.

I'll write him instead. Just because Beth, Mom, and now the heavens are against me, not to mention the phone company, I'm not giving up.

10/4

Maybe I will give up. I cannot write this letter. I've tried 8 times and each time I sound more stupid.

Dear Dave,

I hated you a couple of weeks ago. Actually, it wasn't until a couple of days ago that I stopped.

So why am I writing you now? Am I a complete hypocrite?

Don't I have any self-respect left?

I'm going to just send him something . . . a message . . . without a long, sappy letter. I'll tear off a boxtop from his favorite cereal. I'll send him my most prized South Dakota buffalo postcard from the bulletin board over my desk. No, he doesn't deserve that.

Dear Dave,

You don't deserve this postcard. You realize that.

But I just wanted to let you know I miss you, too.

Love,

Courtney

Can't believe I just wrote on the back of this postcard.

Now I have to put it back on my bulletin board and I'll have to look at it and remember how stupid I sounded. Must try again. Must wait a few more days, though, so I don't look overly eager. Guys like that.

Have you ever wanted to take a day back and just call a "do over"? Today was Courtney the Candidate Day.

"Do over! Do over! Do over!"

It was like a battle I read about once. Where the army gets beaten down and broken and has to summon every ounce of courage it has just to get out of the foxhole.

My Own Private Waterloo? Saving Private Courtney?

It started out nicely. Mom has this real gift for making theme food when we have big events. Cello-shaped Jell-O the day of Alison's recitals. Sneaker-shaped cookies for Bryan's track meets. So this morning she put this hammer-shaped pastry in front of me. I kept staring at it. I had no idea what it was, but I couldn't tell her that. So I just ate it and said thanks. Then she asked if I wanted another gavel.

"Mom, I'm not going to be a judge!" I laughed.

She laughed, too. "I know, but do you have any idea how hard it is to bake a vice-presidential seal?" She held up this flat, round, semiburned, semifrosted pancake. I tried not to take it as an omen.

First thing at the assembly, we all had to state what we wanted to do for the school and what we were all about. I told everyone that I would be a really good vice president because I'm the middle child and am used to getting along with everyone. (I stole a bunch of psychological-profile lines from Beth.) And I mentioned all the things I wanted to see happen. No more dissecting animals in science class, no more using the leftover animals from science class in the cafeteria, etc. (Okay, just kidding.) Anyway, I think my speech pretty much rocked.

After each of our speeches, we had to take questions from the audience. The first one was asked by Mrs. Martinez—I guess it was supposed to be a warm-up question: "Please state your full name."

So I stated my name. Courtney Smith. That's full enough, right? I mean, you don't hear Al Gore or George W. Bush running around dishing out *their* middle names. It's just a "W."

So then we had these questions from the audience; there were mikes set up, like this was a TV talk show. One of the Desaulnier twins stepped up to the mike, and asked: "Courtney, I heard a rumor about you, and I want to verify it."

"Sure thing," I said politely. As I recall, I even *smiled* at him. There was no dirt on me. I'd been completely celibate lately. I wasn't worried.

"Okay, um . . . is it true your middle name is V.D.?"

Everyone started laughing, like it was the most hilarious thing they'd ever heard. My face got hot, I could feel it. This was so dumb, this was the last thing anyone needed to know or talk about, it was just this attempt to find something to laugh at me about. And how did he know this? Was it from Dave? I could feel this onion ring I ate for lunch expanding into a giant circle in my stomach, strangling me like a big squid. Hanging me out to dry.

"V.D. is not my middle name," I said.

Oh my God. I sounded like a public service an-nouncement! "Don't identify me by my sexually trans-mitted disease, I'm a person deep down inside."

It was *awful*. Everyone started laughing really hard. Mrs. Martinez called for quiet—when it finally happened, it didn't last long.

"Is it true you put the *vice* in vice president?" the other Desaulnier shouted.

All of a sudden the Tom came up behind me, I guess to support me. He put his hand on my back. I was kind of glad, if you want to know the truth, because I felt really stranded out there. Then he put his *other* hand on my back. I waited for him to offer me a backrub. Here we go, I thought. The beginning of the end.

But he didn't do anything except press once and let go. Then he stepped forward and said, "If everyone would just give Courtney a chance to talk, we could wrap this up."

I was so shocked I nearly fell down. The Tom being nice? With nothing in it for him?

I cleared my throat. "My middle name *is* Von Dragen," I said. "And I realize these are very unfortunate middle initials. But I can't help it, it's an old family name. And I don't think anyone should be punished for their name, or for anything else they can't control, like their background, or their skin color, or their sexual prefer-ence." Oh my God. I was on quite the tirade.

But somehow it worked. Everyone totally cheered me, and started shouting "Courtney for V.P.," "Courtney V.P. Smith!" instead of V.D. I was convinced everyone was going to vote for me. A landslide victory, or, more to the point, a rockslide victory. People get killed by rock-slides.

Maybe they were just applauding because they felt sorry for me. I mean, I applauded for the other guys, and there's no way I'm voting for them.

Hmmmmm.

Of course when I walked through the halls today, I heard it all. "Hey, it's Courtney STD." "Look, here comes Courtney the Dragon." "Yo, Dragon Lady, what's up?"

Like you can rise from the ashes and all, and every-one will applaud that, and everyone pretends to believe in being so open and supportive of people who are middle-name-challenged. But when it comes right down to it? You'll get teased. Humiliated. If anyone can find fault with anything about you, they'll point it out.

Beth and I went to the girls' soccer game with Jane after school to watch her superstar little sister play. Jane kept going on and on about what great hair accessories she found at Miser Mart. Beth and I kept looking at each other in amazement. What is Miser Mart and why in the world is Jane shopping there? She was sort of slipping on her pledge to never be caught dead or alive in anything nondesigner and nonexpensive.

I waited for them to shower me with sympathy. They stole a cup of Gatorade from the team's table for me, but that was about it.

"Von Dragen, huh? Well, *that* sucks," Jane said, clip-ping and unclipping her new barrettes.

"Your face was so red," Beth said. "I've never seen it like that."

I think I need more supportive friends.

P.S. I'm calling in sick tomorrow. Someone just called and asked if I would be willing to give a health services speech on sexually transmitted diseases, since I'm out of the closet on having one.

I'm sitting at my computer and I have a paper due in 12 hours that I haven't started yet. So I got up and put on my favorite Steve Maddens with my pajamas.

I'm like the "before" picture. In a computer magazine. I need a makeover and also a memory upgrade.

Time for another pledge: I will never leave a paper until this late again.

Would it be so awful if I didn't go to college? I'd save Mom and Dad a lot of money, for one thing. I'd start working at an interesting place sooner—get out of the food service industry. If smoothies and shakes qualify me for anything.

SLIGHTLY LATER ...

Took a short break to do some reading. I just threw down my fashion mags in disgust.

Why is everything "bubble gum" color this year?

Nail polish. Perfume. T-shirts. Etc.

We are a Bazooka Bubble Yum Society.

Was there ever a spearmint year? Sugar-free cinnamon?

Don't they realize that for those of us with reddish hair, this is a complete and utter disaster? I have enough problems without trying to wear baby *pink*, okay? Like, for instance, freckles. Not getting completely fried when I step out the door. My lips are chapped beyond recognition.

And what do I get to put on them? What is selling at every stupid gas station and convenience store? PINK LIP BALM.

Where is the "balm" in that?

Realize I am going slightly insane over worrying about election results.

Whoa. Just got off the telephone. First the Tom called to say he thinks we will win. "You already won," I told him. "It's me that's running."

"We all win if you win," the Tom said. Being disgustingly nice. Then he had to go back to his date.

Then Alison called. She is so homesick or something it's scary. She started crying the second she heard my voice. "Is Mom there?" she sniffled.

"No, she's at her book club," I said. "What's wrong? Didn't you make first chair? Did you have a bad recital—"

"My whole life isn't music!" Alison yelled. Funny. Then how come she spent all her free time reading sheet music and risque biographies of famous composers? Why was she even at this college that specialized in having a great Music Dept?

"So what else is going on?" I asked sort of awkwardly.

"I can't . . . it's just . . ." She was totally fumbling.

So I told her about my Life Skills course and how dumb it was so I had nothing to offer her, but I could tell her what an idiot I was during my speech, and she could relate, what with the Von Dragens being her ancestors, too.

"But who's Tom Delaney?" she asked.

I forgot how totally out of it Alison could be. Her social circle was more like a semicircle. Shaped exactly like an orchestra.

By the time we hung up she seemed much better. I guess she just misses us.

8:45 A.M.
I WON!!

10:01 A.M.
The euphoria has worn off. The reality has set in.

I have to be vice president with Tom Delaney, the boy who has scored with every single member of the senior class. Or at least everyone on the student council. And probably some of them in the student council office. On the student council desk. Gross.

Should I wear garlic around my neck? Or pepper spray?

"Don't you see what's so perfect about this? You're the only one who can resist him," Beth said. (I'm in study hall now. Studying. Just look at me go.) "Because you're not even into good-looking guys. You have, like, no effect on them."

"Excuse me?" This was my best friend talking?

"I mean—they don't affect you," Beth said, laughing.

"No. Not nearly as much as I'd like them to," I said.

"Shut up. You could go out with any guy you wanted," Beth said. "Forget about Dave. Start looking!"

"I told you, Beth—I'm not dating anyone this year," I said.

"Okay, okay. How about just . . . you know. A *fling*?"

I raised my right eyebrow. "And those always work out so well for you."

"They do," she argued. "At the time, anyway." Then we both laughed.

10/10 a/k/a "The Longest Day of My Life"

Okay, so: Beth and I were at Truth or Dairy for our dreaded/favorite Saturday shift. We like it because we work together. We hate it because everyone from school comes in, and Gerry's always there, hovering, telling us to "scoop now and chat later."

Then all of a sudden at about five o'clock she dropped her scoop and said, "Oh my God. Courtney. Look who just walked in."

I figured it was her Crush Du Jour. But it was Dave. Walking through the door with that saunter of his. Wearing jeans and a new T-shirt.

"What is he doing here?" she asked, as he made his way toward the counter. "Don't they make smoothies in Boulder? So why does he come here?"

"Because we're the best," I said. "We use organic fruit and—"

"Shut up with that promotional crap!" Beth practically screamed at me. "It's because of you, stupid."

When he looked at me, I ran into the storeroom to get a fresh tub of frozen yogurt out of the freezer. But after I picked it up, I didn't feel like going back out there. What would I say? What would he say? My hands were getting all sweaty. What if I dropped his smoothie? What if—

"Courtney, what are you doing back here? We have a *line*." Gerry had his hands on his hips, doing his outraged stance. He's big on not having lines.

"We needed more nonfat plain."

"We did?"

"There's going to be a run on it," I said.

He shook his head. "Never mind predicting what people want, Courtney. Go take their actual *orders*."

I shuffled back out to the front. Beth was standing right under the giant arrow that said, PLACE ORDER HERE. And Dave was standing across from her, gazing up at the menu on the chalkboard. Like he doesn't know all the drinks already. He came here a hundred times to pick me up or hang out with me.

I tried to step in front of Beth and take his order. She wouldn't let me. She's only 5'1" but when she gets her stance going, you can't move her. I guess she thought she was protecting me. "What can I get you?" she mumbled in this sort of angry voice.

"Hi, Beth." He smiled at her. My knees kind of buckled. It could have been the giant tub of yogurt, so I set it down on the counter by the minifridge we have up front. Dave was all by himself. That was weird. I tried not to read too much into it as I rearranged spoons in all the fixins' bins.

"Hey. I got your letter," he said, looking at me.

"You wrote him a *letter*?" Beth almost shrieked.

"So, do you want the usual?" I took the opportunity to move in front of Beth. I tried to smile at Dave, but I was having a really hard time looking him in the eye. It was impossible. I was afraid I'd see something in there I didn't want to see.

"Um. Yeah. Coconut Fantasy Dream," he said. "Extra—"

"Fantasy?" I asked.

He laughed. "Coconut." Like I didn't know.

"I'll make it," Beth said.

"No, I'll *make* it," I said, pushing her aside by the fruit bin. Did she really think she could step in and steal my ex-boyfriend just like that? Just because I *dreamt* it?

"It's a smoothie. I'm Truth today," Beth said, very self-importantly. "See this apron?"

"But the Coconut Fantasy Dream has yogurt in it, so technically, it's Dairy." We have arguments like this a lot. Usually only when good-looking guys come in. "It's both, and in case of a tie we look to the possession arrow." I stared at the dangling arrow above our heads. "Oh, look at that—it's pointing at me."

"Courtney. *Don't* make him a drink—after the way he treated you?" Beth said. "Unless you're going to make it really bad—" We sort of started shoving each other. It was like we were seven years old again and fighting over who got to ride the teeter-totter.

"Girls? Is there a problem?" Gerry materialized at my elbow like a housefly. "Does it really take two of you to make one smoothie? Courtney—help the next person in line."

I mindlessly scooped pralines and cream into sugar cones for an older couple. Dave hovered in front of the ice-cream tubs.

"So I heard you got caught in that hailstorm." He

sipped his Beth-made CFD. "Where were you going?"

"Um . . . that new mall complex thing. In Broomfield? With the new shoe pavilion wing?"

"Oh." He seemed sort of disappointed.

"Yeah. Got some great deals," I told him.

"Grant says you're the new vice president. Is that true?" Dave asked.

I nodded as I started putting together a Hot Fudge Fudgorama. "True. I just started a couple of days ago."

"*Why*?" he said in this really snotty tone. "You never cared about that stuff before."

I ladled about an extra pint of hot fudge sauce onto the sundae. "Why are you even *here*?" I said.

"Courtney. Don't be like that," he said with this soulful soul-patch look. Wait a second. Isn't that what he said the last time we spoke? "I came to apologize. I came to talk to you. I came—"

"To get a Coconut Fantasy Dream. And in case you haven't noticed, they do make smoothies in Boulder. Maybe not as good as ours, because they're all chains. But there's a place on the Hill, I think, and they have bagels, too, I went there once with my dad when he visited—"

"Courtney! I came here today because of your letter," Dave said. "Didn't you *want* me to?"

"Courtney? Is there a problem?" Gerry asked, pausing in front of me, holding a wet dishrag in his hand. "I need you to clear some tables." He shoved the clammy dishrag at me.

Just then Bryan walked in. He said he was there to catch a ride home with me and Beth. When he saw Dave standing there talking to me, he started glaring at him. As if he was creating this force field or something.

"So I should probably go. I have a lot of studying to do," Dave said, backing away. "Hey, Bryan."

"Yeah. You should go," Bryan said angrily.

My little brother had never stood up for me before. And I hated him for it. Instantly.

I ran over to the window and pretended to be cleaning off tables as I watched Dave get into his cute red Jeep and drive away.

"Hey, Bryan, what you did just now? That was really nice," Beth told him.

"Nice? You were totally rude!" I said.

"Give me a break. You've been moping around the house for almost two months. You've been completely miserable. And now when you're starting to feel better? He shows up here for a smoothie? Come on!" Bryan scoffed. "He probably didn't even pay."

"He did, too," I said.

"Okay. But did he *tip*?" Bryan asked. "I bet he didn't appreciate the service. Just like he didn't appreciate you." He dropped a dollar in the tip jar. "Thanks, Beth. This is great." Then he turned to me. "That's how it's done, okay?"

"What do you know?" I said. As if Bryan knows anything about romance.

So we were all standing in the parking lot, about to

get into Beth's car, when Dave drove up again. He pulled into the spot beside us and looked at me. I could tell it was time for The Talk. Or *a* talk, anyway.

"Beth?" I said. "Go ahead and give Bryan a ride home. This might sort of take a while."

I'll write the rest later. My fingers are starting to cramp.

THE BIG TALK CONTINUED ...

So Dave drove us to my house and we sat in the parked car, beside the curb. I didn't think I should ask him to come in. That would be like revisiting a major crime scene. Mr. Novotny was outside his house raking leaves—or, rather, "leaf." He's completely obsessive about his lawn. When a leaf falls, he runs outside to rake it— unless there's a Broncos game on.

So Dave started out by saying *again* how ridiculous it was that I was on student council.

Finally, he admitted that it was all about the Tom. "I can't think about you and Tom," he said. Is that why he drove down to Truth or Dairy? Because he's jealous?

"What are you talking about? You don't have to," I said. "There is no me and Tom. It's not like we'll be dating."

"I *know* Tom. You guys will be dating within a week."

"No way," I said. Anyway, weren't we sitting there having this Talk so that *we* could get back together? Or what was the point?

"Look at all the other girls he's gone out with," Dave said.

"I don't have time. And anyway, I'm not *other girls*," I said. "I'm me."

He considered that for a second. Like perhaps it was true? But it wasn't necessarily a good thing.

Maybe I don't love Dave. Maybe I hate him.

"So anyway," I said. "What did you want to talk about?"

"You know. Stuff. Like maybe us getting back together."

My heart pounding, my palms sweating, etc. Panic attack.

Then he went on. "I mean, I don't think we should get back together right now. But I think three or four months from now—"

I couldn't believe it. He's *obsessed* with time lines!

"You have these really warped ideas about time and space, you know that? You should be in like a science fiction movie—not my life."

Was that a great line or what?

I got out and slammed the door. My coat got caught on the window, so I tugged at it. The zipper ripped the Jeep's plastic window like it was a worn-out reused Ziploc bag.

Why did I do that?

Why did he drive down to *say* that? Am I supposed to start planning? Counting down the next four months? He took off down the street. Mr. Novotny was shaking his rake at me, so I ran into the house, lay on the bed, and started crying.

I hate this!

Naturally I called Beth instantaneously. She had the nerve to not even be home yet. Of course Bryan wasn't either so I figured they must have stopped at Safeway or Blockbuster or something. So I called Jane; her mother said she was out shopping for some more new hair accessories to match her new eyeglasses. I wish I had her life. I wish I had anyone else's life right now. Even Oscar's.

Had my first student council meeting today. Since I'm new, I'm supposed to have all the new ideas. I couldn't believe how slowly it was going. Also, the Tom *has* no ideas, unless they're about sex. Mrs. Martinez said how wonderful it was to have me on board and asked what my first issues would be.

I casually mentioned how we should assume a leadership role, for the middle school. The closest one in our district is called Goat Mountain Canyon. Don't ask me how they came up with these names. The area is growing too fast and they ran out of cool names about thirty years ago.

"I like the mentor concept," I said. "We should help build their futures." Because with the name Goat Mountain Canyon, they're going to need help building self-esteem.

It sounded good, really. I didn't have much of an idea where I was going with the whole thing when I started, but then I remembered this article I'd read about how a teacher challenged his students to read a certain number of books. If they did, then he vowed to kiss a pig on the lips.

Do pigs have lips? Maybe this teacher kissed the snout. Anyway, there was a picture of him in the paper, because the kids read even more than he challenged them to, and I thought it was great.

So I suggested we challenge the Goats. A peer pressure sort of thing to see if they could read as much as we did.

Nobody cared about the kids reading the books, but they got really excited about some dare that we'd have to pull off or be subjected to. All of a sudden there was a vote and now if the middle-school kids read 3 books on average each by November 15, we all have to spend a night sleeping on the roof of their school—Principal "the Duck" LeDucque, too. Wonder if she knows yet.

After the meeting the Tom wanted to talk to me. "We need to go over some details," he said.

I bet, I thought. "Like what?"

"Well, you and I have to go over to the middle school and run this by the principal," he said. "What time is good for you?"

I couldn't believe it. He was so not putting the moves on me. Of course, it was only my first day.

When I got home I told Mom there was no way I could go to Nebraska because I was on student council and was too busy planning stuff like Homecoming and now I had this book-challenge thing going.

She did this paper-rock-scissors thing, only it involved school-politics-family. Family won.

Crap.

This diary has been certified by the FDA to be dairy-free***. Wheat-free. Gluten-free. Whine-free. (Okay, maybe not, but definitely wine-free. Alcohol-free in general.)

What the heck is a gluten, anyway?

What I really need to focus on is staying boy-free.

This is a Boy-Free Zone. Imagine signs like that at school. Perhaps I could institute this as my first official vice-presidential act.

*** Not to be confused with free and clear.

You could say I'm throwing myself into my work lately. Beth called in sick, so I was bored and got really into making up new drinks. I made one for Gerry called the Wheatgrass Whirl when he dropped by. "I love it!" he cried.

"You do?" I couldn't believe it.

He poured himself a large glass of water and downed it. "Oh. Well, the drink is *horrible*, yes. But what I love is your initiative! Keep inventing drinks, Courtney, and I'll keep trying them until you get it right. You're such an asset to this place."

What a boss. "Okay then," I said. "I've been thinking we should take the Coconut Fantasy Dream—" my voice nearly choked on the name— "off the menu. And put this on instead."

See? I'm trying to move on, I really am.

I put orange juice, coconut, and frozen strawberries in the blender, then raspberry sherbet. But that was too much like a Sunrise Strawberry Supreme. So I tossed in some pineapple and a little plain yogurt.

"I'll keep this under review," Gerry said. "But Courtney, don't even think of getting rid of the CFD. It's our most popular drink. A business survives—no, thrives—on *hits*. So . . . hit me again." Gerry laughed. "Get it? Hit me? Hey, speaking of gambling. Did I tell you I went to Central City and played the nickel slots last night?" The man lives *so* dangerously.

When I'm old enough to gamble, I'm starting with the quarter slots. Minimum.

For some reason this whole experience led me to the Taco Bell drive-through on the way home at 9:00. I got all the change from the tip jar and pooled it into a value meal (people are so generous). Only I ordered the wrong kind of gordita. I don't eat meat often enough to know the difference between gorditas. Ended up with way too many vegetables. Not the point at all.

No wonder I can't sleep.

Why didn't I drive up to see buffalo instead? Much healthier alternative. But probably too dark to see them.

Agh! Nightmare. Just went downstairs to grab some toast and juice. Still in my PJ's. Mom and her gang are all sitting at the kitchen table, drinking coffee, laughing, telling stories, talking about their kids. It's her Saturday routine.

I heard them on the stairs and paused as I heard my name mentioned. By Mom.

"Courtney says she'll never date anyone again. No, wait—she says she won't this entire school year," she told her pals.

Everyone started laughing. What is so *funny* about having a little integrity?

"We'll see how long that lasts," Mrs. Brell snickered.

"Even if she won't date them, they'll want to date her," Mom said.

"Well, of course, I mean, look at her," Mrs. Lebeau said. "Her skin is so lovely. And her figure, and that copper red hair . . . I wish Mark would ask her out."

Gross! So much for wanting breakfast. Mark Lebeau? Is she insane? He's a sophomore, and he's skinnier than I am. He's also incredibly rich; they have a mansion practically, the biggest house in the neighborhood, and they have parties where they actually valet-park cars (but Mom makes us walk because it's so close).

Anyway, why do Mom and her friends want to talk

about us? Why don't they talk about themselves and their own dates or husbands or whatever? Probably it would be boring, but at least it would be about them.

I'm going back to bed.

So Mom got us all digital pagers. She and her friends went out shopping Saturday after their coffee fest and had technological breakthroughs. There was a big special; buy 2 get 1 free. She was acting like she was doing this for us, but it's her thing. She's obsessed with phones, or not answering phones. She said the pagers are part of our new call block program. More like cell block—we're only allowed to receive one call a day, if we're lucky. I *want* to get calls.

It's almost like she used to date a telemarketer and that's why she hates them so much. They're just people with fast, annoying voices and a habit of mispronouncing names. What's the big deal?

Anyway, besides the pagers there are all these codes we have to use. And we have to punch in about 100 numbers to even reach her at work.

So there I was in the middle of math class, watching Rick Young at the blackboard. All of a sudden I started to get sort of hot. You know. Like I was attracted to him. There was this sort of buzzing sound under the desk, and I felt palpitations.

I never really liked Rick Young, but you know how your body sometimes has this will of its own, genetic needs, looking for the best mate, just like species in the wild, etc.

Then I realized it was my pager. I had set it to vibrate

by mistake, instead of turning it off like I usually do in class.

It wasn't Rick Young, it was Grandma. She was checking to see if I got her Halloween card yet.

Damn. I thought in this weird way it meant I was ready to think about dating again, that I could be attracted to someone besides Dave. Apparently not.

I can, however, receive messages with up to 50 characters.

Hi, it's me. Courtney's Beth friend. (She used to say that when she was little, because she had a slight lisp. It became my nickname. That's the history, okay?) We're waiting for Courtney, who's only taking the longest shower in history. We commandeered her journal as punishment. We're going out tonight to celebrate her new role as vice president. I think it would be great if there was a coo and she took over Tom's job. But he'll never go for that, because he has to be the center of attention.

I guess I don't have much to say, so here's Jane. I hear music. I'm going to see what Bryan's up to.

This is Jane. And it's "coup," as in taking over something, not "coo" as in lovebirds whispering sweet nothings.

I kept a diary once. My mom found it and read it and got all worried because I had all this stuff written about *horses*. I loved horses. Not in that way, just—you know, I was 7. And she made me go to this kiddie psychologist and act all this stuff out with a My Pretty Pony and a Fisher-Price Barnyard and a Barbie. I swear, I'm not making this up. Ever since then I've been very reluctant to write stuff down.

All I wanted was a horse. To take lessons, wear those tan jodhpurs, carry a whip crop (which I'd never actually use). They thought that was twisted. So why did they rent me all those horse movies and buy me all those horse books?

Anyway. Now that I have a chance and a place to write in that my mother will never ever find, I can make a confession.

I still have my plastic Secretariat stashed in a shoe box under the bed.

So *ha ha*, Mom.

Courtney, back to you. By the way, I'm really glad you and Dave broke up. You might not be, now. But you will be.

Cannot believe my journal was like . . . violated.

But the Jane thing explains why she keeps insisting senior class trip in spring be to a dude ranch.

Oprah did a show today on dealing with the mother-daughter relationship. Mom was unfortunately home with the flu and saw it. She put on a coat and rushed down to the bookstore and nearly bought out the mother-daughter section (is there such a thing?). She tried to give me a reading assignment when I got home.

"Mom. We get along *fine*," I said. Except when you're going ballistic about phone calls and insisting I just *try* the veal cutlet.

"What?" she said. "I can tell you're thinking something about me."

"I wasn't," I lied.

"Tell me," she said.

"Okay, well, I was just thinking how sometimes you don't understand why I don't want to eat meat. I mean, you understand, but you think it's just a temporary thing. And it isn't."

She nodded. "I did think it was a phase—at first. But I can see you're dedicated. Most of the time. I was just wondering whether your decision to not eat the lamb shanks I cooked that night last year . . . was a rejection of me."

"No," I said, thinking back to that momentous night when I decided to give up meat. Should I tell her that the mint jelly didn't help matters? "I just don't want to eat lambs. Or sheep. Or other things that walk around on legs."

She smiled faintly. "I wish you wouldn't phrase it like that. But okay. So what other issues do you have with me?"

"I don't have any issues. Period," I said.

"Are you sure?" she asked, like she *wanted* me to hate her for something. I don't. I wish she spent more money on herself and that she would lighten up sometimes, and that she'd go out on a date once more in her life, but I couldn't help her with that.

"I'm sure, Mom," I said. "Just relax. You're doing great." I gave her a little hug and then ran upstairs to my room. Escape!

So now she and Alison have been on the phone for like an *hour*, and I can't call anyone.

It's unlikely I'll have a breakthrough. A complete breakout, maybe. I'm sitting here staring at a stack of college catalogs and applications. They should come with complimentary tubes of zit cream.

"My most meaningful life experience was . . . (a) filling out this application, (b) taking the SATs, (c) getting my first computer, (d) deciding I'd rather manage a Truth or Dairy for eternity than fill this out."

Gerry keeps talking about expanding. And Beth and I have to not laugh, because the fact is that since he opened the shop a couple of years ago, he has to have gained about 30 pounds. He has this belly, the kind guys get when they drink a lot of beer. But with him, it's from coconut and kiwi and strawberry. The other day he said he could really see himself growing. We started to laugh, but then he added, "as a businessman and a pillar of the community."

"Do you want to be a chain?" Beth asked him. "Do you want to be all over the country?"

"Well . . . define *chain*," Gerry said.

"More than one," Beth said. "Linked together? With standardized napkins and recipes."

"I'd like to be a Colorado chain. Yes. I see that," Gerry said, as if he'd just called the psychic hot line. "But I want to grow in a healthy way. You two will help me, won't you?"

Afterward Beth and I went into the storeroom and just cracked up. "Sure we will," Beth said. "We'll put *diet coconut* in your smoothie."

"Don't forget the sugar-free strawberries," I said.

"He thinks fat-free is like . . . all there is to it," Beth said. "He's so wrong."

Most people are.

This is too embarrassing to write down. But so is almost everything lately, so here goes:

Mom asked me to pick up food for Oscar on the way home. So you know there's this pet shop at the other end of the strip mall from T or D—it's called Pet Me, which has all these weird connotations, so I used to think it was a sex-toy shop. I went in there after work and found the chow Oscar eats. I picked up this humongous bag—Mom only buys it forty pounds at a time. I was dragging it up to the cash register, clutching it like I would a small toddler, when I heard this familiar voice.

"Need some help carrying that? Hey, how's your dog?"

It was Grant. He had a Pet Me Staff shirt on, plus one of those weight lifter's belts. An interesting look. I'd forgotten I ran into him that day at Walgreens and told him about Oscar.

Well, okay, so I guess he wasn't *following* me. He works here. That's why I kept seeing him in the parking lot after work. I am such an idiot.

And that's why he has such big shoulders, it's not from sports or dietary supplements. It's from hauling forty-pound bags of pet food and cat litter.

"You know, we offer free delivery," Grant said. Now he tells me. "But I can help you with that now, if you want."

I was tempted, but sweat was running down the front

of my shirt, about to mix in with the kibbles and make my own gravy.

I was so embarrassed I paid and ran out to the car. I realized my Grant-as-stalker theory was a bit off the mark. It isn't all about me and Dave. It's all about me being self-centered and oblivious and stupid.

Had to sprint into T or D today from parking lot. I'm so embarrassed about what I said to Grant. I skipped my class with him, my major life issue today being to avoid Grant. So humiliating. Thinking someone is stalking you when they work in the same strip mall. Not only that, but I've droned on and on to him about Dave, I'm sure he thinks I'm completely unbalanced, crazy, deluded. No wonder Dave would break up with me. All I could think about last night when I was trying to fall asleep was how Grant probably called Dave and told him what happened. Instead of giving him this cool image of me going on with my life, no problem, Dave has a new image: me thinking I am the bomb, that everyone wants to go out with me . . .

Okay, enough about that. Gerry wants to send me to some management class being held in a few weeks. He says he's following up on his idea of branching out, the store being a very successful concept, smoothies being trendy and all, while ice cream never goes out of style.

"Don't tell Beth," he whispered to me by the supplements. "She doesn't have management-quality potential."

She'll be crushed. I'm sure.

I'm calling her tonight to tell her, so she can deal with the pain privately.

I asked Gerry if it could wait until next summer—when I'll quit. He launched into some speech about the ideal smoothie shop, how the serving of cold fruit drinks side by side with rocky road is the yin/yang feng/shui harmony of food service. Completely off his rocky road.

"I'll pay for the class, and I'll pay you overtime for the hours you attend the class," he finally said.

Yes!

Something weird is going on with the Tom. I think he has ADD or something, well, especially when it comes to girls. Like he can't *focus* on which one he likes. Today he had three different gifts on his desk and couldn't remember which one he was supposed to give to whom. He kept pushing them around on his desk like he was doing that trick with 3 shells and a nut underneath. I don't know where he gets the money for all this; I guess he comes from money, because I know he doesn't work. I was waiting for my gift. Shouldn't he be giving me presents right about now?

We went over to Goat Mountain last week and issued our book-reading challenge in person (the principal already told them about it). They have two more weeks (plus) to get it done. The kids had a lot of funny questions, like: "What roof are you going to sleep on?" "Can we watch?" "Can we sleep on the roof?" and "Can't we throw cream pies at you guys instead?"

Then someone pointed out we'd be sleeping up there in November and how that's usually one of the coldest months and what if it snowed, wouldn't *that* be funny? I think they started reading as soon as we left the auditorium.

Dave called tonight. He said he just wanted to know how I was doing.

Did he mean that?

I can't believe it's been over two weeks since the last time I saw him. I'm starting not to miss him everywhere. It's nice. He asked if Tom had made a move on me yet. I told him not to insult me. Of course he hasn't, and of course he won't. He's too busy planning whose sleeping bag to sneak into after we lose the Goat Mountain challenge.

Goat Mountain Challenge. Isn't that a Disney movie?

Just woke up. Dreamt that I was sleeping on roof of Dave's house. Kept sliding off.

That was a dream within a dream. Woke up from that one into another one. Turned out I was trying to sleep on Flatirons, rocks with sharp angles, mountains above Boulder. I was up there to spy on Dave, had binoculars and was trying to find his dorm. Strap on binocs nearly strangled me.

Then I realized I was naked.

Oh yeah. I am really over him.

Had a last-minute emergency meeting today to talk about Halloween party at school. A group of students submitted a petition asking us to ban costumes. We can't *cancel* Halloween. I'm sorry. It has these . . . themes. Scary ones.

In the meantime it is only 3 days away, and I have no idea what I can go as. Last year Dave and I went to the party together as Sonny and Cher—and there's no way I can top that. I could be Cher, I guess. But that would be really pathetic, even if in real life she was the one who dumped him.

Maybe I can be a witch. Or wait—a dragon. Since my secret is out. I could go as Princess Von Dragen. Sounds good, but who is it?

The theme of the party at school is Trick or Treat. I have to consider reassigning the head of the social committee. Her name is Laura, and she has no ideas. Period.

Called Alison to see if she has any costume ideas. She was out. She's *always* out lately. So frustrating. She must be practicing for a big concert.

I called Beth. I could have sworn I heard a guy talking in the background, but she kept saying it was the TV and she had to go because she was in the middle of watching a show for a paper.

Jane picked out her costume last spring and wouldn't understand leaving it to the last minute.

I was so desperate I even went to Bryan's room to ask him for help. He wasn't home.

Oscar ran away. He got spooked by all the kids coming to the door and ringing the bell and screaming "Trick or Treat!" at Mom, who was wearing a belly dancer costume. A bit skimpy in my opinion, but she and her friends all went to this Act Your Shoe Size, Not Your Age party this afternoon, so Mom's feeling 8 1/2.

Since I got home from the party at school, we've been looking for Oscar all night—me, Mom, and Bryan. Probably the most time we've spent together since the summer. Mom drove; I ran alongside the car; Bryan kept yelling Oscar's name out the window until he was hoarse.

First we cursed the neighborhood—I mean coursed— on foot, then we drove to all his favorite places: the park, various Dumpsters, the grocery store, even Pet Me. No Oscar.

All the funny things that happened at the party seem kind of insignificant now. But still funny. I found this old costume of Alison's in the attic. She went as a cat a few years ago. Slight problem, I'm a size bigger than Alison, but the leopard material was stretchy and besides, it perfectly matched my new leopard print fuzzy slippers. I looked hot, maybe a little too hot though, sort of like a stripper.

Anyway, Jane was a figure skater, with a dress that had a billion sequins so she sparkled even more than usual and she had awesome four-inch-heel shoes that looked like skates. Beth was dressed as Smokey the Bear, which was really weird because Bryan was a firefighter so we kept asking if they had talked about using a fire *theme*. They kept swearing they hadn't. Bryan kept picking up Beth and pretending to carry her out of a burning building. It was hilarious.

I danced once with the Tom, but people kept grabbing my tail when I spun around and he got annoyed because I was getting more attention than him. Naturally he wasn't in costume. He's too cool for that. Right.

Beth, Jane, and I ran into Grant at the punch vat. He was dressed as a cowboy, he even had those leather chaps.

"You should be on a calendar," Jane told him as she looked him up and down.

"Courtney—I didn't recognize you," Grant said. "You look sort of . . . curvy."

Jane and Beth started laughing. Then Grant was smiling, too, like he was really enjoying embarrassing me for my Feline Stripper outfit.

It's really cold tonight. Seems like it always is on Halloween. Or maybe it's because I was wearing too-thin, stretchy material.

I hope Oscar finds a warm place. I hope he doesn't get caught by that leash guy, either. Crazy guy. Would probably jail Oscar for killing goats, like Oscar's ever killed anything. His food even scares him.

Oscar's never been gone this long before. I was a total mess at school today. I shut my hand in the door when I was leaving Mr. Arnold's classroom, then I almost started crying in the hallway. I think I might have even whimpered. So embarrassing.

Grant was right behind me and grabbed my arm. "What's wrong?"

"It's Oscar. He ran away." I pulled this old crinkly photo of Oscar out of my backpack and nearly started bawling. I took the picture when we brought Oscar home from the hospital after he got hit by the car.

"Oh? Oh no." Grant looked really worried. "Do you have any idea where he went? I mean, can I help you look for him?"

"Why, do you know all the dog hangouts?" I snapped.

He looked sort of hurt. I realized I must have sounded a little harsh and insensitive. Which is sort of typical for me these days.

"I'm sorry, I didn't mean *you* would know. Because you're a dog or something. Because you're not, at all, believe me, I wasn't implying—I just thought, well, you work at that pet shop—"

"It's okay, Courtney." He put his hand on my arm again. "I know you're upset. Do you want to look for Oscar after school together?"

"I can't—I have to work," I said. So he promised he'd

131

look around his neighborhood and call some people and see if they'd heard anything about a sort of gray and brown and black mutt.

I was making a Silly Sherbet for a kid today (I hate when people order it and say "Sherbert", like "sure, Bert!") when there was a slobbery thing on the glass in front of me. You know, like spit, smeared back and forth over the sherbet tub? I hate when people let their kids actually drool while they're deciding what to order.

"Listen, kid, do you mind?" I started to say.

Then I saw this gigantic tongue. Something gray—fur—OSCAR!

I leapt over the counter and hugged him before Gerry could tell me it was all a giant health code violation waiting to happen, and before Oscar could lunge for this little boy's strawberry sugar cone he was eyeing, mouth open.

Grant followed me outside. I was so grateful I thought about hugging him, too, but he didn't exactly have that huggable look. "Where did you find him?" I asked.

"By the pasta factory. Apparently he got sort of mesmerized by the flashing red ziti-shaped lights. You know what? I think maybe he needs a new diet."

"More pasta?" I asked.

Grant shrugged. "Maybe. It couldn't hurt."

I played with Oscar's frayed green collar. I didn't really see how new food could clip years of brain fur off his life, so I didn't say anything.

Funny. Dave never knew where to find Oscar.

Grant just drove around, block after block, for like *hours*.

I opened the door tonight to Mr. Novotny from across the street. The yard/Broncos-obsessed man is about 60, bald, with big square glasses. And very, very single as a direct result, as far as I can see.

"I don't know who Dave is," he said, "but would you tell him to stop calling?"

How embarrassing. Not only is Dave calling me (*why?*) but he's getting Mr. Novotny.

"Is Dave the guy with the red Jeep? Who used to be over here all the time?" he asked.

"Um . . . yeah," I said. Thanks for reminding me. "We broke up, but—"

"Good. And I don't want you to get back together with him!"

"Um . . . really? Why not?"

"His driving is frightening. I've star CSP'ed him at least twice."

*CSP is this cellular direct connection to the state police. But it's not a *verb*.

Mr. Novotny has a cell phone? Mr. Novotny has road rage? I've never even seen him leave the perimeter of his yard. He mostly mows his lawn on a riding mower that he's painted in Bronco colors. Except in winter when he shovels snow with a Broncos snowblower. And puts up his orange-and-blue Broncos season lights on the front porch.

"Well, um, what did he do, exactly?" I asked.

"His parking is atrocious. But that's not the point," Mr. Novotny said. "He shouldn't drive so fast. He nearly hit me on the Field Captain."

"Mom?" I called over my shoulder. Save me!!!

She came out and explained how she'd asked for this new phone feature to block out calls. When MegaPhone installed it, they must have crossed the lines or something. It's called call control plus. Which to me sounds like queen-sized panty hose.

"More like control minus," Mr. Novotny grumbled.

"No wonder we haven't heard the phone ring in a few days!" Mom laughed. "But I kind of enjoyed the vacation from the telemarketers. Sorry for the inconvenience— we'll get it taken care of tomorrow," she told Mr. Novotny.

It's weird we didn't notice, but I guess I've been busy. Plus, I always call Beth—it just works that way between us.

That wasn't good enough for him. He wants us to run a really long extension cord across the street so the phone will ring in our house instead of his. Mom pointed out it might get run over. She apologized over and over.

Mr. Novotny finally said he'd ignore his "land line" and instead use the cell phone he carries on his mower. And uses mostly to report bad drivers.

I called Dave to see why he kept calling. He sounded very annoyed. I asked if I was bothering him or interrupting him—maybe he was studying for an exam or something. He said no. Then he asked why I was calling him now, why I was bothering to take the time out of my busy schedule as vice president. Huffy like a bike.

135

I told him maybe if MegaPhone fixed our line, his calls wouldn't keep going to Mr. Novotny's house and maybe I'd have a clue he called.

"What are you talking about?"

"Our phone. It's been broken, and we didn't know. And um . . . this is really funny. Do you want to hear it?" I started laughing.

"Wait a second. Mr. Novotny?" Dave laughed. "The Broncos mower guy? *He* heard my messages? No. Please tell me that isn't true."

"Why? What did you say?"

"Never mind, what did *he* say?"

"He's called the police about your driving. You went too fast and it somehow messed up his lawn ornaments, sent all the whirligig things into a whirl."

We kept laughing and talking about how weird Mr. Novotny was, how he was the kind of person who might flip out one day. But instead of everyone saying afterward that "he was such a nice neighbor," they'd probably say, "the signs were there all along."

Then Dave said, "So do you want to come up here or not?"

I do. So I am. Tomorrow.

But why is he always calling and writing just when I really am *not* thinking about him? Like, at all? He has this sixth sense or something.

Room 314. Welcome to *My* World.

I'm sitting outside in the hall, thank you very much. Dave's not here. If I sit outside and wait, I'll miss him—too many entrances and exits.

I look ridiculous.

People are playing hacky-sack around me.

I know, I'll call him and tell him I'm waiting outside . . . in the car . . .

Hold on, I hear laughs in the stairwell. Sounds like Dave.

It isn't. There's a guy with pink hair approaching Room 314. I think he just said my name.

It's Chad.

LATER...

Still can't believe what happened. Puff Chaddy knew me because Dave told him I was coming plus he has a photo of me over his desk. (!) (Dave, not Chad, that is.) Chad said he'd been looking forward to meeting me. Then he put on some really loud music, a rapper I didn't recognize, so loud the walls were shaking. He got out his lighter. I thought he was going to smoke something, but he lit this patchouli incense and lay on his bed and said he had to unwind after organic chemistry.

"What's organic about that?" I tried to joke.

He didn't get it. Or he wasn't in the mood to laugh. Dave came back about ten minutes later, and he tiptoed into the room, took my hand, and we tiptoed out. I asked him what was going on with the Puffster. Dave said he's incredibly driven to be a doctor.

"Dr. Puff?" I said. We laughed really hard. Dave showed me around the campus and when we ran into Alicia from our school, she didn't even blink, she was just totally excited to see us together.

It all seemed normal, except when the afternoon was over and Dave said something about studying and it was clear I was supposed to leave and clear we were still just friends. I tried not to make a crack about his 6-month plan. I failed.

I left in a huff. I was halfway out of town when I realized I was the one being rigid, sophomoric, etc. So I went back to apologize.

Stood in hallway outside his room, staring in at Dave and some girl. He was laughing and having the time of his life.

Unreal! I am so unbelievably hurt. I can't even write any more. I can't even call Beth or Jane and tell them. It's humiliating. Was I the 3 P.M.–6 P.M. date?

Is that part of the New Plan?

I cornered Grant after class again. I needed more insight. A guy's perspective. Plus, I was hoping he could identify the suspicious laughing girl in Dave's dorm room.

"So why would he ask me to come up, say he missed me, etc. and then be with some other girl?"

"Maybe she's just a friend?" Grant could tell he sounded lame, so he didn't go on. He didn't even put any heart into the comment.

"Do guys like torturing us or something?" I asked. "I mean, is it sort of *fun* deep down?"

"No, of course not," Grant said. "But people get, um, conflicted I guess. You know, when they want two things at once?"

No, I don't know. You either want something, or you don't. Like me and *dating*.

Speaking of conflict: the Tom keeps buying stuff for our office: plants, pens, posters. Things Beginning With "P" For $100, Alex. I think this must be out of frustration that he hasn't scored with me yet, or else he's really into interior design and can't admit it.

Still really mad at Dave. Jane and Beth and I are going shopping tonight; screw sitting around and waiting for the phone calls.

No messages? What is his *problem*? Too busy laughing with his 6 P.M.–overnight girlfriend?

The Tom continues to amaze. Today we had this table in the cafeteria set up so that people could sign up for Homecoming activities and buy tickets for the party, etc. While we're sitting there (after he eats 4 cheeseburgers in 5 minutes) he's working on his college apps. And every single (pretty) girl that comes up gets the same question, as he bats his so-long-I'm-jealous-of-them eyelashes. "Hey, could you help me with this section? What do *you* think are my three best qualities?"

The girls take it really seriously and crouch down by the table and offer suggestions like, "You have a strong leadership quality," and "You take charge," and "You're responsible," etc. etc. blah blah blah. Then after a while he switches to asking what his three best features are, whether it's his eyes, or his perfect nose, or his amazingly huge . . . ego.

He offers the really pretty girls back rubs for helping him, and our student council table turns into one of those 5-minute back rub carts at the mall. And I have to listen to him say, "Well, you know this works a lot better skin-on-skin" about a dozen times while *I* do all the work, sell tickets, make change, etc.

Finally, the bell rang. I thought we'd get out of there but then remembered there was one more lunch period to go.

"So I could probably help you with your applications," I finally offered. "You don't need to give me a back rub."

"Oh. Yeah?" He actually looked sort of interested for a second.

"Sure. I mean, if you want to thank me, you could just go straight to the full-body massage," I suggested.

The Tom stared at me, beyond shocked. "Oh. Well, actually, my applications are sort of like . . . done. But, um, thanks, Court." Then he ran off for a glass of chocolate milk.

What? After all these years I decide to flirt with him, and he has the nerve to not flirt back?

I complained to Beth and Jane about it after school.

"He probably doesn't want to mess up your . . ." Beth stopped, not able to think of the right word.

"Presidential relationship," Jane said. "Like he messed it up with Jennifer. If you leave, then he'll have to find another VP, and he's already had two—"

"He hasn't *had* me yet," I said. "And we're not going out, I don't want to go out with him. I just think it's ridiculous that he doesn't even try."

"Maybe he's not attracted to you," Jane said. "It happens."

"We're talking about the Tom," I reminded her.

"Oh."

Nobody said anything else. It was too awful to suggest Tom wasn't attracted to me. That would be like saying I was dead. But I bet he's into that, too. He's attracted to everyone, alive or dead, except me.

Then I realized I was being ridiculous. My whole life I'd wanted the Tom to avoid me. So he was. So what? He's a ridiculous person who looks good, and that's it. It's time to focus on something besides boys.

Got in the car and drove to see the buffalo. Stared over the fence at them. Life would be better if I were a buffalo. They all look alike, more or less, and even if they don't, they mate regardless of looks. Of course I'd have to wear the same hooves every day.

Finally talked to Dave today. As it turns out . . . that girl he was laughing with is his resident adviser in his dorm. She came up to talk to him because everyone is getting kind of concerned about Chad. He's been experimenting in his chemistry class a little too much, making things that aren't on the lab assignment, etc. Everyone was worried he was stressed out and making something dangerous. So they did an Organic Intervention.

Turned out he was trying to invent a new line of organic hair coloring. He's so stressed because he doesn't want to be a doctor, he wants to be a stylist. His parents won't accept that he wants to be a hair doctor, not a surgeon.

"Does CU offer a cosmetology degree? Or is he going to drop out?" I asked. And did you have to laugh so hard with her, when I was standing in the hallway? We used to be able to *sense* each other's presence.

"Come up tomorrow," Dave said.

"I can't," I said. I told him about the Smoothie Seminar I'm attending tomorrow night. Then we laughed again.

It's 7:30 P.M. and I'm sitting in the Matterhorn Conference Room at the Rockies Swiss Alps Inn (does that strike anyone else as redundant?). There are about 26 other people here for the smoothie management course. We're going around the room bonding over questions like: "If you could be one additive, what would you be and why?"

I tried really hard not to laugh. One guy said he'd be creatine. I said I'd be ginseng—no, wait—bee pollen. Because more people are allergic to that.

"If you had to classify yourself as a drink, are you milky, tart, smooth, or citrus?"

"I'm a milky tart," I said. Because you know. I can't really be *defined* by these *limited* terms.

Claude (a/k/a Clod), the director of this panel (a/k/a Claude the Fraud) is giving me these looks, like I'm dissing the juicing phenomenon and ought to be run through the blender myself.

We're moving on to motivational skills now. I'd better pay attention. I can't even motivate myself, much less someone else.

We all went out to eat tonight—student council "we," I mean. The Tom insisted on going to this place near Golden because they serve Rocky Mountain Oysters, i.e., bull you-know-whats. He probably thinks they'll make him more virile, like he needs help in that department.

Maybe he does. Maybe that's what all this is about. A desperate attempt to—

Nah.

Anyway, it was sort of fun. I told him it was a horrible thing to eat. Did he know how tortured a bull had to feel when he had them cut off? Did he think that was right? I asked how he'd feel if someone cut off *his* major organ.

The menu consisted of things that turned my stomach. Chicken fingers. I always picture a poor chicken's pathetic little claw being fried up. Who wants to order fingers, anyway? Are we all cannibals at heart? At least they call a wing a wing, except for Buffalo Wings. I bet buffaloes wish they had wings. They could fly away and not become burgers.

I ordered a salad. Oil and vinegar. Very boring, shredded carrots and a radish the only saving graces. "You've got to loosen up," Tom said as he glanced over at my meal. "Live a little."

"Oh, yeah? What do you suggest?" I asked.

He held his plate toward me.

"No. Thanks. Really," I said.

We made final arrangements for Homecoming and

Tom said not to worry about cost. This should be the biggest, best ever. There's plenty of money in the budget, so we can go ahead and have a parade, a rally, a dance, etc.

"The theme will be . . . coming home," Laura actually said. She needs a brain infusion.

I wonder if Dave is coming home for it. I want to know, but I don't want to ask. Of course he *should*. He's close by. But it might be too much of a commitment for him, making that long drive.

Grant asked if I wanted to eat lunch today. Of course I did. I mean, why wouldn't I eat lunch, I practically live for the meal. But with him? Just us? The concept sort of freaked me out, so I ended up saying something really stupid. "What section would we sit in?" I asked.

"Do you really care?" He sort of laughed at me.

"No. *No*," I said.

"We'll sit outside," Grant said. All cool about it, like it was no big deal. So it wasn't, I told myself. It's not a date or anything—just a sort of calorie-sharing plan. "I'll go get some sandwiches and then meet you by the fountain, okay?" he said. "Ham and cheese okay?"

Not okay! The fountain is where Dave and I used to eat lunch. I know where every bird dropping is. But what could I do? I went outside and waited. Looking pathetic. All the still-together couples stared at me like I was clinging to the past like bird crap to granite.

Grant came out with our lunch. I took out the cheese and then the ham. I basically had a mustard sandwich going. On white. I tried not to let him see me toss the ham and cheese part, but he noticed.

"Oh, I forgot," Grant said. "Dave told me you don't eat that. Sorry."

"It's okay," I told him. "Don't worry about it."

"So when did you quit eating meat and cheese?" Grant asked. He kept looking at his sandwich like he shouldn't eat it. "After a really bad sub?"

"*No*," I said, laughing. I loved the way he made a joke out of it.

We talked about Oscar. Grant asked how we named him, and if it was from my intense love of the Academy Awards.

"I don't love any awards show," I said. "What are you talking about?"

"And the Oscar goes to . . ." he kept saying in this really deep fake announcer voice, and we both kept laughing really hard.

Every time he lifted up his straw to use as a microphone, and did this silly pose, the muscle in his dog-food-lifting arm rippled.

Did I just use the word rippled to describe something other than a potato chip?

What is happening to me? Maybe I need to get out more.

Afterward he told me he has a golden retriever and two cats and one of them belongs to his grandmother who lives with them now and the two cats don't get along blah blah blah. It wasn't boring, it was just that I stopped listening at some point because I had to focus on myself. I was starting to feel like (a) I was on a date, and (b) I really wanted to be on this date and (c) I was attracted to Grant and (d) I would be breaking my rule really soon if I kept this up.

Wrong! No pledge broken. This wasn't a date. This

was a lunch that didn't taste very good. This was a discussion about pets. Animals, my real passion. And I'm not interested in Grant.

But then why did the phrase "Pet Me" keep going through my head?

Stupid Question of the Day:

"There's this long-distance company that offers free ice cream when you sign up. Are you guys in on that deal?"

Beth and I looked at each other and then back at the guy asking. "No. But there's a pay phone outside the fabric store over there."

He went outside and nearly got run over by one of the Guccheez Pizza (they were Gucci's but they got sued) delivery guys. He leapt to the sidewalk, fell, and scraped up his hands. I went out to see if he was okay, and I saw Grant in the parking lot, so I waved to him. He smiled and waved back. I started thinking how I feel about Grant. (Pet me! Pet me!)

But there's no point. I'll go away to college. He won't. Or maybe he will, but not to the same place. And then what? Forget it. I'd probably just end up blowing him off like Beth did, and he doesn't need to get rejected by both best friends.

"Could I get a Band-Aid or something from you people?" the guy yelled up at me. "Or does your store offer nothing to the public?"

Whoa. Talk about an unhappy customer. I brought him back to the store, made him a Mind Soother (with antianxiety herb additives), put extra ice on his hands, and let him use Beth's cell phone. And stopped thinking about Grant.

Those stupid kids at Goat Mtn. read all the books by November 15. Now I have to sleep on the roof with the Tom. All night.

We were supposed to do it on Friday night, but this Friday is Homecoming (duh) and next Friday is Thanksgiving (duh). So much for using a calendar. They said we could do it now, or wait for a Friday in December, which sounds like a really bad idea. So we're camping on the Goat Mountain school roof tomorrow night, and we'll get to miss our early Wednesday morning classes and our teachers will supposedly understand.

But will they understand the hell I've gone through, sleeping outside with the Tom? I can't imagine. I don't want to imagine.

"I have one of those sleeping bags that wraps around you like a burrito," he said to Laura, our social committee director, after our meeting broke up today. (Still need to fire her, by the way.) "It's big enough for two."

"Really?" Laura asked. "What do you mean? It's a tortilla? That's kind of gross."

"No, it's just that style. We can roll up together," he said.

"Oh." She shrugged. "We can?"

Yeah, and then we can all vomit over the edge of the roof.

There's going to be Mrs. Martinez, Principal LeDucque, and the rest of the student council up there.

Does he seriously think he's going to score, on a roof, surrounded by people, as part of an "increased literacy" program?

Sexual literacy, *maybe.*

"Up on the roof . . ."

Someone keeps singing that annoying tune. I'm going to kill him, whoever he is, even though he has a good voice and can pull it off.

The Tom is pretending we're camping. He's telling ghost stories. The scariest part of the story is how bad he is at telling it.

It's so cold out here. And the air has that smell, like snow is coming. Bitter and sort of damp. Whose idea was this, anyway?

Oh. Right.

From this school high atop Goat Mountain (which is in reality a small hill, on top of which is this rectangular building and a bronze goat sculpture), I am looking down at a billion identical subdivision houses. A sea of lights. They're not very attractive, but the fact they have lights makes them look really warm and inviting on a night like this.

I just looked at my watch. It's only seven o'clock.

I think I should have worn more clothes. Why was I trying to look good? Should have worn 3 pairs of long underwear.

Have to stop writing. Hand is becoming frostbitten.

The first snowflakes just started falling.

"So Courtney. This was *your* idea." That's how Principal LeDucque greeted me. She was wearing a big knit Avalanche hat. While she was glaring at me, snowflakes started hitting her eyelashes. She had a megamug of coffee in her mittened hands.

"At least we're getting good publicity," I said. A few reporters had shown up. We'd been photographed earlier, when it was still light out. Cars full of Goat Mtn. Canyon students kept pulling up to check on us—and laugh. Their parents even laughed.

"Yes, I guess so," she said. Then she smiled. "And it is a good cause." She put down her mug and started rubbing her hands together as she gazed up at the snowy night sky. "I'm afraid we won't get much sleep tonight."

"No, probably not." So I suggested we go ahead and have our next student council meeting now—after all, the entire student council was up there. We huddled by the big square heater vent and talked about how not to dare the middle school again.

"So I suppose it's time to turn in," Mrs. Martinez said. "If anyone is too chilly, let me know. We can call for additional supplies."

Everyone seemed okay. I couldn't admit to her that *I* was the unprepared one. I looked around for my sleeping bag. Turned out that it was right next to Tom's. He had me on one side and Laura on the other. He was explaining his sleeping bag to her. Actually she needed some help with her own. She's a bit slow on the uptake. On any uptake.

"You guys might want to, you know, *move*," I suggested. Because I didn't want to be around when they wrapped their burrito.

"We have a great spot," Tom said. "What's the problem?"

"N—nothing," I said. My teeth were already chattering. I got into my sleeping bag and zipped it up. They were talking for a while, but then they both drifted off to sleep.

Snow was still coming down. I pulled my hat tighter on my head and scrunched into a ball. That didn't help. Mom bought budget sleeping bags for us, and I swear, this one was only rated to 60 degrees. It was designed for sleeping on the floor of a well-heated family room. In front of a roaring fire in the fireplace.

I heard snoring and looked over at the Tom. I didn't have a choice. I told myself that if he woke up, I'd have to deal with whatever happened. And maybe it wouldn't be so awful. If anything happened, it would be meaningless and vapid, not like anything real.

I really slowly and carefully (hands frozen, didn't work very well) unzipped my sleeping bag. Then I unzipped his. Sleeping bag, that is. Then I tried to zip them together but my shirt sleeve got caught in the zipper and I couldn't get it out. I must have spent half an hour struggling with that cheap icy zipper. I was muttering and swearing and Tom still didn't wake up. So I moved a little closer to him.

And then the next thing I knew I woke up with snow on my face and I was spooning right next to Tom.

I heard him say, "Good morning." I quickly checked to see if my clothes were on. They were. I said, "Good morning" back, and he turned around like the devil had spoken.

"Oh! I thought you were Laura," he said.

"Sorry," I said. "My sleeping bag is so thin. I sort of . . . had to."

"Oh. Well, whatever." He got out of the sleeping bag and stretched his arms over his head. The sun was coming out, and the air felt a lot warmer already.

"This is so *cool*," Tom said. We sat on the edge of the roof, ate donated donuts that were dropped off by someone's parents, and looked out at the sunrise.

I kind of felt like we were in that IMAX *Everest* movie. Only we didn't have to hike up more than Goat Hill, there was plenty of oxygen, and nobody died.

"This was harder than I thought," I told Tom. "I didn't really think about the fact it would be November."

"Yeah. But we made it. And you know why? You're a survivor, Courtney. Just like me." Tom slapped me on the back. "Don't worry. I won't tell anyone how you came on to me last night."

"I didn't come on to you," I said. "I was trying to avoid hypothermia."

"Okay, fine, whatever you say." Tom took another donut. "*We* know what really happened."

I have to run to school now—I'm late late late!

Beth and I were at work today. She kept disappearing on me. Like she'd start to go outside, sneaking through the supply room, and then she'd stop. And come back. But finally she did go outside, so once I had a free second I went to find her.

She was standing outside, with her back pressed against the wall like she was trying to hide. And she was SMOKING.

"Have you ever done something that you thought maybe you shouldn't be doing?" she asked me.

"Hel-lo. Like *smoking*?" I almost screamed. What were we, Truth, Dairy, and Nicotine now?

"I'm sorry," she said. "I can't help myself."

"Are you serious?" I said. "That's all you've been talking about lately, how much you *can* help yourself and control your life."

She just took another drag.

"Beth! Snap out of it," I said. "You don't need to smoke. Remember all that junk you said about steps and addiction? And those disgusting black grilled-lung photos and—I mean, do you realize how many *hours* you spent lecturing on the evils of smoking?" I tried to grab the cigarette from her hand, but it was impossible.

"I still believe in that," Beth said. "But sometimes you have to be yourself."

"Yeah. Whatever." I can't believe her!

Beth again. Courtney tries to hide this now, but we found it under her computer keyboard. This needs to be documented: we're all going to a big party shortly, at Keith's house. Homecoming! Whoo-hoo. Like I care. I can think of many things I'd rather be doing. (Not smoking. Not smoking. I slipped up, but I've confronted my feelings and faced my problems head-on and that won't happen again.)

Tom made this point of personally asking Courtney and then repeating himself like 6 times. So we're all calling it a date. Except Courtney. She's claiming to be only going because we are and because it's good for the student council for her to be seen in public. And because Dave might be there, and she only saw him for about 5 minutes today, and he said he'd "see us tonight," but I could tell he wasn't coming.

Anyway, come on, if Tom asked me 6 times? I'd know he was interested in me. Especially since they bonded after their Winter Wonderland roof adventure.

Courtney is spending a lot of time getting dressed when you consider she hates the Tom. What do you think, Jane?

Look, Beth—*you* dressed nicely when *you* went out with the Tom.

I didn't know I was going to go out with him. We didn't go out, anyway. We made out in like . . . the coat closet.

And on the street. And outside the house. And on the sidewalk.

He was a good kisser. What can I say?

More than that!!!

Tom said things. Nice things. About my hair. My sweater. Junk like that.

Your sweater? Oh, gag, I think I'm going to be sick.

You don't get it, Jane. Nobody gets it until it happens to them.

Exactly why Courtney is wearing her favorite shirt and that flowered mini that looks so good on her. Oops, time to shove this back where we found it so she doesn't kill us this time.

Chapter Number 57
In Which the Tom Lives up to His Name; Or Not

Yes, I'm home early, and I can't believe Jane and Beth stole this to write in *again*. I'll get them both their own blank books for Christmas. Hold on, let me write that on my list. Okay, so I'm back.

What was I thinking? Was I just dressing up to look good because Dave might be there? He wasn't there. I pretty much knew he wouldn't be—like he was too cool now to go to a (long-distance) high-school party. That sort of made me mad, but I sort of expected it. Anyway.

Did I just want Tom to notice me, like those guys said? I guess so. He'd been acting like I was an asexual ugly freshman. (Okay, like I *still was* one. Because it's true, the apple doesn't fall far from the divorce tree and when I was 14 I had braces and a bad attitude and custody hearings to attend.) And you can't come on to every straight female (like he even asks whether they're straight or not) in Colorado and *not* come on to *me*. So okay, I was flirting a little. But did that give him the right?

We were standing in the kitchen, near the fridge. We were laughing about the sleep-a-thon, how we should have volunteered to sleep in the bookmobile, no, wait, drive it. Or we could have sat in one of those tanks with the bull's-eye and gotten dunked.

He hopped on the counter and said he'd like to see me in the dunk tank, like in this challenging tone, as if I deserved it because I've been so impossible to deal with lately. I sort of leaned against him. Then I got the idea that wasn't it. It was more about me in a wet T-shirt. And I sort of liked that he thought that. Maybe I'm just desperate and need someone to notice me, maybe it was time to end this self-imposed no-dating rule. I mean, I technically don't eat meat, and the other day I had another of Oscar's hot dogs—okay, that was a really bad analogy. But you can't be pure wheatgrass, meat free and clear, all the time.

But wait, that slip doesn't even count, because hot dogs aren't even technically *meat*.

Okay, so back to the story. So then Tom said the party was lame and we might as well go do layout together, it would be more fun. He meant yearbook layout; I knew that, but he didn't *say* it like that, and besides, he was sort of playing with my hair when he said it. I felt like everything was leading to one foregone conclusion. So when he said he was going to the coat closet I said I would go with him—of course. Because I was thinking about it, and at least with Tom, it wouldn't *mean* anything, it would never be a dating relationship for more than a few days anyway, so I wouldn't break my rule.

When I walked over to the closet, Beth was dancing in the living room, waving her arms frantically. I think she had too much coffee at work today. It was really weird. She was just hanging with Jane, not trying to hook up with a guy or anything. Totally unlike her.

The closet was packed, unlike the party. We sort of bumped into each other when we went for our coats.

Something could have happened right there. But it didn't. We put on our coats and then he walked me to my car and I kept waiting for him to do something. And it was really cold. So eventually I felt really stupid and I just got into the Bull and drove home. Alone. Him not following me. He probably went back into the party and picked up someone else.

What the?

Would it be so awful to make a move on me? Since when is playing with someone's hair *okay* if you don't plan on kissing them later? Maybe he wasn't playing with it, maybe he was taking a tortilla chip crumb out of it. Still!

What am I talking about? It's Tom. *The* Tom. Like I *care*.

Dave called this morning. He started off by saying, "Yes, is Mr. Novotny in, please?" That was pretty funny. He said he was sorry about not meeting me at the party the night before. I was glad he hadn't been there—he would have seen me get blown off by Tom, which is something that's like never happened before. Ever. It would have been really humiliating. Then again, if Dave had been there, I might not have wanted anything to happen with Tom. Not sure.

Then Dave said he really wanted to talk to me, but it was hard with all those people around. And he knew I was leaving town for Thanksgiving in a few days, so could I come up there?

But when I got there, he had nothing to say. Maybe it was because Chad was giving this other guy a haircut and a platinum bleach in the room. We didn't exactly have much privacy.

"Then, Dave," I said, trying to be mature, "why did you call me?"

"I miss you?" he said with a sort of shrug.

There was this unbelievably awkward silence. I kept playing with this tassel thing on his bedspread. He's had this blue-and-white-checked bedspread since he was 8. He's the only boy I know who has one at all in his dorm room—not that I know a lot of guys with dorm rooms, but. You get the picture. I think his was actually a tablecloth once upon a time.

"So do you want to get something to eat?" one of us finally said. We ended up walking over to the Hill. We were leisurely strolling along when I saw an empty storefront and a giant sign: DENVER'S VERY OWN TRUTH OR DAIRY—COMING SOON TO BOULDER! WATCH THIS SPACE!

How could Gerry do that to me? I mean, how could he do it without telling me—and Beth? I hate when people do things without telling me! What is he thinking, anyway? Okay, we're a popular store, but I think what makes us special is there's just one of us.

Dave was psyched, though. Can't wait for his favorite smoothie to be back in town.

We walked around, and it seemed like it used to be between us, but it wasn't. We were all limp-like, droopy, lifeless. Especially when we went to say good-bye and gave each other this half hug. Our relationship (if we still have one? If we have one again?) needs a high-energy power powder infusion. The more bee pollen, the better. Any kind of pollen.

Maybe we should just let it die.

So Dave called tonight while I was in the middle of my new Turbo Yoga (it's the pumped-up version of relaxation) tape and told me he's been seeing someone. He was trying to tell me all day, but he didn't know how. That's why he didn't go to the party—he had to go back to Boulder to see her. "But it's no big deal," he said. "It isn't anything serious."

I sat there clutching the phone wondering why I'd ever given him my control plus code. This felt more like out-of-control. Sweat was running down my wrist. I started writing things with it on my forearm, like YOU SUCK. But I ran out of sweat.

I hate being told important (ugly, horrible) news on the phone! I hate it whenever and wherever I get it. Especially when it's from Dave.

I asked if it was that resident adviser person. He said no, it's someone else, a sophomore. Then he actually started to *tell* me about her, like I wanted to know, like I'd asked. I hung up as soon as I could.

I flashed back to the night in August out by the BBQ when he told me he wanted to be free and clear. Is dating someone else being free and clear?

I had him so close to a burning hot fire that night. Why didn't I *do* something?

I HATE HIM!

When I got to work, completely dragging my heels, fifteen minutes late, I asked Gerry why he hadn't told us about the new store. He said he wanted to surprise us—also, the lease almost fell through. But he said more exciting details would be coming soon. I asked if he meant more stores. He said we were going to start offering more choices "within the Truth or Dairy tradition of good fruit and good food."

How about the Truth or Dairy tradition of crazy owners?

Jane picked me and Beth up from work. We went to this new coffee place where we could be guaranteed privacy—it's in one of those new developments where they don't even have street names yet. We barely found our way in. But Jane has this nose for coffee, she could probably find her way to Starbucks if it was located in a landfill. Survival instinct.

"We shouldn't even be here," Jane said. "We should be somewhere we can meet guys. Because that's what you need, Courtney—a new guy."

"No, I don't think so," I said. I started building an anthill of raw sugar on the table.

"Listen to us. Dave's seeing someone else. So should you," Beth said.

"I can't," I said. "I told you guys, I don't want a relationship this year. I'm not looking for a boyfriend."

"Come on. Don't be silly." Jane tossed a stirrer at me.

"You said that in the heat of the moment—"

"Ahem, you have it in writing," I said. "I wouldn't have written it down if I didn't mean it. That's why I'm vice president with the Tom, that's why—"

"Courtney, come on. It was funny when you said it," Beth said. "Remember? We laughed about it. I told you about the advantage of flings, remember?"

"It wasn't funny to me," I said. "I was completely serious. Look, you guys. I appreciate what you're saying. But could we just complain about Dave and not talk about me? Because I'm not changing my mind. I never change my mind once it's made up. Can I have a sip of your latte?"

Beth and Jane looked at each other.

"What?" I said.

"Oh, um, nothing. Here." Beth pushed her cup toward me.

"So do you want to eat lunch together?" Grant asked me today.

Unbelievable! I glared at Grant. He *knew*. He had to know. And he never mentioned a word to me about Dave seeing someone new! And I was supposed to be nice to him? And he expected me to wait until he got his lunch, then eat a mustard sandwich, and suffer through his sympathetic looks and I-knew-before-you sighs?

"I can't believe you," I said. "I thought you were like . . . my friend. Sort of."

"I am. Sort of," Grant said.

What? Was he my friend, or wasn't he? "With the emphasis on the sort of," I said.

"What's that supposed to mean?" he asked.

"I don't know. Like I told you a hundred times, Grant, I don't understand guys. Especially you!" I said.

"What are you talking about? What did I do?" Grant asked.

I glared at him. I was seething. All that overly dramatic stuff because I felt so incredibly humiliated and he had a part in all this. Then I said something I probably shouldn't have.

"So now I know why your nickname is Lake Superior."

He stared at me like he'd never heard that before.

"It's because you're so like . . . gray and vast and *cold*. You sink ships. You don't care about anyone!" Then I stormed off down the hall. Then I realized I forgot my courier bag, which was in the student council office. I hate not being able to exit when I want to.

I ran up the stairs. Tom was sitting at his desk, being presidential. He was writing checks to pay for the New Year's party we're planning—we need to make deposits on all this stuff.

"Courtney, I thought you left," he said.

"I wish," I said.

"Where are you going again?" he asked.

"Nebraska," I said. "I told you ten times—"

"Where in Neb—" he started to say.

"Yeah, well, *bye*!" I ran out of there before he could talk to me about the fun vacation he had planned.

Thank God it's Thanksgiving (is that redundant or what) vacation. I really really really really need to get out of here and away from all these jerks!

This will probably be illegible. I am writing with ice-cold hands—and gloves on. So is Bryan, in a notebook. He won't show me what, though. I asked and he got all snippy about it.

"You're not keeping a *journal*, are you?" I asked.

"Shut up," he said. "Anyway, if you can, why can't I?"

I don't know. He just can't.

We're sitting in the Taurus. We're stuck. The Bull is not going anywhere. And there is a certain contingent in the car right now who think this is all my fault: Bryan, Mom, and Oscar.

Never mind that there's a severe blizzard happening. That the road is closed now. The problem is that we skidded off the road because I was going too fast for the conditions and also I was thinking too much about Dave and last Thanksgiving and Dave and this Thanksgiving and what I was doing with my life, and how he was seeing someone new but that didn't upset me as much as my fight with Grant, but why did I have to keep thinking about Grant, plus I kept eating jelly bean after jelly bean, I was on quite the sugar rush.

Next thing I knew there was this 18-wheeler in front of me and I swerved to miss it and I went off the road in this long skid and thwacked into a snowbank. There's a billboard for a Motel 6 in the distance, but no Motel 6. We're way too far from anywhere to walk, as if we could. Lots of other cars are stranded, too—when the blowing snow lets up, it's going to be *hours* before anyone comes for us.

Mom is surprisingly calm considering that we're going to miss the pie schedule.

"Courtney? More cheddar?" she just asked me, holding out a giant bag. Mom's excessive planning comes in handy because of the stockpile in the cooler.

"Mom. No," I said. "I don't want any cubed cheese. Can I have a carrot?"

Bryan's crunching on wheat wafers. "If we had a cell phone, this wouldn't be happening."

I can't believe he had the guts to just say that!

Mom's arm is twitching where it's resting on the back of the seat. "We'll be *fine*. All those other people with cell phones can call *for* us. All right?"

Bryan isn't having any of it. "No one's going to call. They can't even see us, Mom. The snow is covering our car!"

"Well then, get out and brush it off," Mom just said. "Make sure you uncover the tailpipe."

We're running the heater once every half hour. When you get stranded in a blizzard you have to remember to clear the tailpipe or you'll die. Either way it feels like we could die, though, if you want to know the truth.

Bryan's trying to open the door, but it's nearly frozen shut. The wind is blowing so strongly that ice is forming on the inside of the windows. Bryan wrote HELP ME in the frosted glass with his finger. The cranberries in the trunk are definitely frozen, and I don't want to even think

174

about "all the breads for the meal" that I spent hours baking last night.

"I'll take Oscar," Bryan just said. "He probably needs to go." We gave him a glass of snow about an hour ago. I'm watching the two of them. Bryan is kicking the tailpipe so hard it might fall off. Mom's arm is still twitching. Oscar raised his leg and it seems frozen in that position.

Uh-oh. There he goes!

No one's going to believe this. I don't believe this. I'm writing this in the bathroom, for one thing. That's pretty strange. But I didn't want to turn the light on and wake Grandma, and I can't sleep, and every other room is taken.

So here's what ended up happening this afternoon after I jumped out of the car to save Oscar from running away (and let's face it, he wasn't scared this time—he was just sick of being in the car, like we were—and decided to strike out for freedom).

First of all, the snow was too deep. Oscar's legs got stuck. Bryan and I picked him up and put him back in the car. Then we started clearing off the car. Bryan took the sides and top; I was clearing off the back. It seemed silly to clear snow off the bumper stickers, but hey—if you're going to be stranded, why not give people a political message to read while they creep by, going 20 MPH, totally ignoring your plight?

I was brushing off the TRUTH OR DAIRY—FRESH FROM THE FARM AND GARDEN! sticker when all of a sudden this new, souped-up black pickup with gigantic snow tires pulled up behind our car. Someone was coming to help us! I was so excited.

Then who gets out of the truck? TOM DELANEY.

"What are you doing here?" I think I asked. A really dumb question. I know.

"Driving to North Platte to see my dad for

Thanksgiving. Wow. This is wild, huh? You guys stuck?"

"Why did you stop?" I asked. "I mean—"

"I saw you," Tom said. "Plus I recognized your car. You have that Truth or Dairy sticker. And that tofu sticker. You have to be the only one in Nebraska right now with that sticker. Where are you going?"

"To visit our grandparents," I said. "And the Von Dragen cousins. Remember?"

"Oh, you're going to the V.D. homestead." Tom smiled.

"Ha-ha," I said as I glared at him.

"Chill, Courtney. I'll help you move the car."

We tried, but the Bull wouldn't budge. Plus we only had a couple of ounces of gas left. So then Tom ends up offering to take us all to the Von Dragens. We can go back and get the car after the storm, he says.

So then the only problem is how we're all going to fit. If we're going to fit. We all had to sit up front, even Oscar. Good thing Mom is so tiny. But they made me sit next to Tom. I was crammed against the gearshift. A wet and thawing Oscar was lying across Bryan's and Mom's laps. All our luggage was in the back, under one of those black plastic truck boxes.

I thought of how Beth said the hailstorm was a sign that I *shouldn't* get to Boulder and reconnect with Dave. So then was this a sign that I was supposed to hook up with Tom? I'd have to call Beth.

We got to my grandparents' four hours after we were supposed to be there. Because of the snowstorm, everyone was worried sick about us, and it was a big party when we finally arrived. We kept thanking Tom—me, Mom, Grandpa. Grandma made him drink three hot chocolates. He tried to leave, but everyone insisted he stay for dinner—it was all hot (and overcooked, I was thinking) and what was one more place setting for the boy who'd saved our lives, etc. etc. etc.

"Thanks for everything, but I should really get going," Tom said at about nine o'clock. "My dad's expecting me, so—"

"Don't be ridiculous. In this weather? You're staying the night," Grandpa declared.

"But it's only fifty miles—"

"Do you know how many people's last words have been 'It's only fifty miles'?" Grandpa asked. "Listen, son, I've seen more accidents on this stretch of road than world wars."

I thought to myself, two? More than two? Because I think Tom can take his chances. The thought of him staying here is really bizarre. But I didn't want him to get into an accident, and the snow really hasn't let up yet. So he's sleeping downstairs on the sleeper sofa.

I was trying to fall asleep, but then I realized what I thought was a stomachache from Grandpa's pre-Thanksgiving meal—Cornish game hens, "a little warm-up for the big bird!" he said (no wonder he and Grandma sleep in separate beds)—wasn't going away, and was in fact another kind of ache altogether.

So now I'm sitting in the bathroom, looking at a box

of tampons that for some reason has all of the warnings in French.

Question: Why does Grandma still have these and how old are they? Wouldn't she have gone through "the change" about 20 or 40 years ago?

Question: Do tampons expire?

The box is warning me of *Syndrome de Choc Toxique*.

Why does *death* sound good in French? Like an exclusive all-night dance club.

Question: Why would anyone ever want to go to www.tampax.com? And what links would it have? I sort of don't want to know.

Dear www.tampax.com: Are you there, God? It's me, court364@netcom.com.

There are a bunch of prescription bottles in here, stacked like cans at the supermarket. All my grandparents'.

Don't let me get old.

And don't let me write in my journal in the bathroom again. Extremely depressing.

THANKSGIVING MORNING (pre-poultry)

Oh God. I thought I'd noticed this weird vibe with Grandma and Grandpa. Like maybe they were a lot more interested in each other than Mom said. So I was in the bathroom for a little while, so I was contemplating the Tampax box. Did they think I wasn't coming back?

I walked back into the bedroom and they were like . . . making out. On the bed. Completely oblivious! Completely about to have sex! Grandma's needs *completely* being met.

So I ran downstairs, totally freaked out. And I ran right into the sleeper sofa and toppled onto the Tom, knocking my shins really hard against the metal frame, and falling onto him.

He opened his eyes and said in this Austin Powers voice, "Hello, hello, what do we have here?"

I only took a second to see whether he had as much chest hair as Austin Powers. His chest was bare. And tan, like he went to a salon and had a fake bake.

I leapt off him immediately after that and sat on the recliner. It was so embarrassing, how could I tell him? But I told him. My grandfather would probably be his idol now, but what the heck. I said how it was weird because they hadn't slept together in a long time, and they actually had been sort of cold to each other the last time I saw them.

He said it was probably the Viagra Effect.

"Is that a science fiction movie?" I asked. Because Grandma and Grandpa being sexy . . . that was sort of science fictionesque.

Look, I *know* it's natural, and I'll probably want to do it when I'm seventy-five, too. But I won't want anyone to know about it!

So Tom went upstairs to the bathroom and came back with this bottle of blue pills. "Just what I thought. Viagra." He shook one into his palm and stared at it. Then he lifted it to his mouth. "Bob Dole would be so proud of my courage right now. These things cost like ten bucks a pop, did you know that?"

I begged him not to take one. He just kept laughing and holding the bottle over his head so I couldn't reach it. We wrestled for a few seconds, laughing hysterically, then the bottle popped out of his hands—Viagra pills went flying everywhere, and we fell on the bed again. This time there was a sort of intense moment where he had me pinned.

But he was more interested in saving the Viagra. He let me go right away so he could scoop them all back into the bottle. Then he tucked a couple into his duffel to take home. "Just in case I start aging really rapidly."

You know those scared-straight movies about kids doing drugs? Like heroin and coke and pot? How about *Teenage Boys On Viagra*!!! This one boy in particular.

We started watching TV and I fell asleep on the fold-out couch beside him. We both had sweats on, it was a completely chaste event, and nothing happened. This is the second time this month I've slept next to him, and it's becoming a really weird habit. Not that unlike having Oscar sleep next to me in bed. A little less furry, a little better breath.

THANKSGIVING AFTERNOON (post-poultry)

Let us *not* give thanks. It wasn't even a free-range hen, like Grandpa promised he'd get me. He went out to the turkey farm and got a fresh kill. "Check out that rotisserie action!" he kept saying, as the turkey turned on the metal spit.

"I'd rather not," I said. I kept staring out the window wondering when the snow would stop.

Remember that movie about people being trapped inside during a blizzard? And they all went crazy and started killing each other? *The Shining*. Set in Colorado. No surprise. Okay, so we're in Nebraska and there are no mountains, but still. We haven't been able to leave the house since getting here, and if we eat any more poultry, we're going to start laying eggs.

Tom is about to lose it. Grandpa started telling him how to "truss a bird." (You'd think Grandpa had a turkey farm his whole life instead of an accounting firm.) I guess we're having . . . what? Roast pigeon tomorrow?

Grandma and Grandpa usually sit at either end of the table, but today they had to sit next to each other so they could play footsie. We're all leaving really soon, I wanted to say. Could you just maybe . . . wait until then? For your love fest?

It is so sad when your grandparents are more romantic than you are.

THANKSGIVING NIGHT

We're all sitting around in the living room trying to breathe. The house is hot and stuffy and we're all so full we could burst. Leftovers IV: The Saga Continues. I just called Gerry and told him I probably won't be back to work on Sunday. He said that he'd work for me. Poor Beth.

Bryan is trying to teach Grandpa how to use his new computer, how to get on to the Internet. Probably so they can go to hotchicks.com together.

"The storm is just not letting up," Tom said. "But I have to get out of here."

"Tell me about it," I muttered.

"Hey, Courtney. You want to come with me?" Tom asked. "I know we can make it to North Platte. But if we want to blow that off, we could just head back to Denver."

I wanted to. *So* badly. But Mom needed me to help her drive home (if she was still going to let me drive.) Finally, there was a break in the onslaught of snow and you could see okay. Tom called the roads hot line and they said the interstate was open again, so the Tom made a break for it before Grandpa made him snowshoe home. This was good news for us, too—the car might get towed to us in the next few days or so.

I walked Tom out to his pickup and thanked him for rescuing us from the snowbank. He gave me his dad's number in North Platte and said to call if there was anything I needed, like a ride back. "Or a meal that isn't turkey," he said, and we both laughed.

Could it be that Tom and I are actually sort of becoming friends?

I wondered if I should hug him good-bye. Or maybe kiss him. I must have been desperate. I sort of leaned against him and squeezed. I felt really stupid.

Right after he left, Grandpa realized Tom didn't give back this antique sterling silver lighter he was showing him. He threw a fit about it. I promised him I'd get it back when I saw Tom at school in a couple days.

I can't wait to be back at school. I can't wait to see Jane and Beth and tell them about the trip and how I slept next to Tom.

There is one person I really am dreading seeing, though. Not because I don't like him, but because I sort of messed up the last time we talked. Maybe he didn't necessarily deserve to be compared to a rocky Great Lake that sinks ships. In fact Grant had been nothing but nice to me before I left, except for that Dave incident. I'd hardly thought about Dave on this trip. Was it Grant's fault he wanted Dave to tell me about what's-her-name in person? Of course, he didn't do it in person, he did it on the phone. Loser.

I started feeling so bad, I decided to call Grant. Of course I couldn't say I was sorry, not really. I started talking about Oscar.

"Oscar tried to run away, but he got stuck in a snowdrift," I said. "He ended up with really, really cold feet and wet fur, but we saved him. Then all he's been doing lately is eating turkey and gravy. Do you think that's okay?"

"He can eat whatever he wants, really. It's just that he has to have his pills."

"Right. Well, seeing as how it was a holiday, I put his pill in a dinner roll instead of a hot dog. He didn't really notice. So, um, what are you doing?"

"Hey, Court—oh, you're on the phone. Who are you talking to?" Tom suddenly appeared in the room.

Haven't you left yet? I wanted to say. "Nobody," I said. "Did you forget something?"

"Yeah." Tom picked up something off the top of the fridge and slipped it into his jacket pocket and then waved. "See you!"

"Who was that?" Grant sounded very offended all of a sudden.

"Oh, just a cousin. One of the infamous Von Dragens," I said.

"It sounded like Tom Delaney," he said.

"Oh. Well, no, it wasn't," I said. Why did I say that? He'll only find out what happened the next time he sees Tom. And then he'll know I lied to him. But how could I tell him I'd slept with Tom the night before—well, in the same room anyway.

Because nobody would believe you'd spend the night with Tom Delaney and *not* sleep with him. No matter how well Grant knew me or Tom. Tom had a certain reputation, and there was a reason for that. And if anyone found out Viagra was involved in the evening, my story would become completely unbelievable. And if anyone found out that I sort of wanted something to happen, that would be even more unbelievable—

Well, Grant was never going to hear that from me. It was too embarrassing. So I sort of changed the subject and started to explain the car skid, and how we had to get towed, but there was a blizzard, etc. (I didn't mention it was kind of my bad driving that did it.)

"So what have you been up to?" I asked.

"Actually . . . I don't know if I should tell you this." Ooh! Intrigue! I thought. "But I've been hanging out with Dave," he said.

Go ahead. *Ruin* my holiday via long-distance. He has some nerve. Can't he be on my side and just ban all contact?

"Well, I have to go," I said. "The gravy is burning."

Grant said how he didn't think I ate gravy. "Of course I don't *eat gravy*," I said. "But I can still cook it."

Actually, neither is true.

Bryan has been on the phone ever since the rest of the Von Dragen clan left. All five of them.

Our family doesn't reproduce well, let's face it. How will the Von Dragen name survive?

By forcing young women like me to have it as a middle name, I guess.

Anyway, Bryan keeps laughing, and he has this bizarre smile on his face. Is he in love or something? He's acting like I've never seen before. I asked him what was up, and he said, "Never mind, you won't get it."

"I'll get it," I said, desperate for some real conversation. "I will! Just try me."

He shook his head. "Nobody will ever get it, so—"

LATER...

Sorry, I was interrupted in the middle of that fascinating update. My mother came upstairs and insisted we go down and join in the giant gin rummy round robin.

Some of this stuff doesn't even sound so bad until I write it down.

After Bryan lost, he got on the phone right away again. I asked who he was calling. He said it was none of my business. Is that rude or what? He used to tell me everything. Sure, he was six at the time, and a horrible liar, but come on.

He must have a girlfriend at home. He doesn't want me to know who she is because he's embarrassed.

This is going to be fun.

Since when does Bryan have a calling card?

Whoa. Just woke up from a dream where I was making out with Grant in storeroom at T or D. It was very intense. Tom was over by the counter, grinding Viagra pills into an additive and putting the powder into smoothies!

"They have drinks for chicks," he was saying. (We do have this one called Ferocious Female that's supposed to help curb PMS.) "Why not drinks for us? It's virility, baby. I call this a Manly Mango Mojo." (Austin Powers influence again.)

Have to stop sleeping on this foldout couch where Tom slept.

Right away.

Made it home tonight. The less said about the trip, the better. Let's just say that Oscar should not be allowed into a car after eating birds at Grandpa's for days on end. Not in the winter, not when you can't open the windows.

As soon as I got home, I called Beth to tell her the whole story.

She didn't seem that surprised. Like this was a normal chain of events??? Grandparents getting it on? Being stranded on I-80? Nearly sleeping with the Tom?

Well, okay, it wasn't "nearly." Close to nearly, though.

"Are you okay?" I finally asked when she didn't even laugh about Bryan keeping a journal and pining away for someone at home.

"Um . . . yeah," she said. Then she said she was sorry she was kind of out of it, she had to work extra hard at T or D because she was working with Gerry, etc. He kept going over all the procedures with her, hovering over the blenders, etc.

"Don't ever get stranded again, okay?" she begged.

It was great to go back to school today. I felt like I was never going to have my life back.

We had a student council meeting to talk about the New Year's blowout. We've done some fund-raising, plus we're selling individual tickets at $3 a pop, and now it's time to reap the benefits.

Asked Tom about Grandpa's lighter. He said he doesn't have it. I called Grandpa to tell him that. There was a message on their answering machine that they've gone to Hawaii for 2 weeks. "*Aloha!*" my grandfather said in this happy voice. I guess he hasn't noticed the missing Viagra yet. Must have enough to tide him over, through the luau with Grandma.

Hey, if I were them? I'd *move* to Hawaii.

Dad called to tell us that his stepdaughter Angelina had her baby last night. It's a girl! Cool. Her name is something like Bellarina. (Doesn't she realize everyone's going to call her Ballerina? And that she'll have to go through life explaining that she's not a dancer? Unless, of course, she becomes one, due to the power of suggestion.)

Dad got all emotional because it reminded him of when we were born and blah blah blah. Then he and Mom started talking about it and they had this really fun conversation and then Mom was crying. Bizarre.

I need to write this down so it makes sense. I was going to call Beth, so I picked up the phone in the kitchen. I heard Bryan's voice and realized he was already on the phone. This must be his dream date, I thought, because Bryan was talking in a low voice. I was about to hang up when I heard the other voice.

I kept staring at the phone as I listened to her. Not getting it, like Bryan always says. But wanting to get it this time.

I stood there unable to move. Completely shocked. Stunned. Deer in headlights etc.

Beth and Bryan were talking to each other about how much they had missed each other, how they couldn't wait for Christmas vacation, blah blah blah BLAH!

"Hey—is someone on the line?" Bryan asked. "Hey, hang up!"

"Gladly!" I said. I dropped the phone and ran into my room and closed the door. My best friend . . . and my little *brother*? Since when?

They're dating . . . they're in love . . . she's the one he kept calling and writing in Ogallala, that's how she knew about the trip before I told her . . . that's why she hasn't been interested in anyone lately, it's because she likes Bryan . . .

I felt like Oscar, standing there with my tongue hanging out, about to go into a grand mal seizure.

She barely just got over having a fling-a-weekend.

He barely just got over Power Rangers.

What the? Talk about *choc toxique*. I can hardly *breathe*.

I knew Bryan had a crush on her, but that's been for decades. Now what? They've been seeing each other—and not telling me. How could they not tell me? Why?

I went back to my computer and sent an instant message to her: "CRADLE ROBBER!" I wrote in all caps, even though that's bad netiquette, I couldn't stop to think about that.

Then I logged off. I didn't want to know what she'd say. I didn't want to hear about it.

Study Hall. Blah.

Beth came over to my locker before school, but I didn't know what to say. Why does her being with Bryan bug me so much? I think it's because they didn't tell me. Why should I be the last to know? Did they think they couldn't trust me or something?

"What's your problem?" Beth said. "Jane's okay with this."

"You're not going out with Jane's brother," I said. "It's different. And I'm not okay with it."

"Obviously," Beth said.

"Anyway, you don't *have* relationships. You have one-nighters," I said. "Are you going to dump Bryan?" Because one depressed person in the family is enough.

"No, of course not," Beth said. "God, Courtney, haven't you noticed? I haven't had any flings this year. It's a resolution I made, to give that up like I gave up smoking."

"Right . . ." I said. "And *that* worked. I saw you smoking last week!"

"I was only doing that because I was freaking out about Bryan!" Beth said. "I wished I didn't like him so much—it was scary. And then the idea of telling *you* about us was even scarier. So I had a couple of cigarettes—but that's it, and I was just trying to escape."

"So when you slip up and make out with some other guy, and totally ruin Bryan's life—"

"That won't happen!" Beth said. Her teeth were clenched like the way the dentist makes you do to check your bite. "I've changed," Beth said. "Just like you."

"I've changed?" I said.

"Yeah. Into a real bitch," Beth said.

Whoa. No one's ever said that to me, to my face. I could see Alison doing it, as a joke. I called her when I got home to tell her what was going on. She wasn't home so I sent an e-mail. She didn't write back yet.

No one ever writes back.

Dinner tonight was hell. Mom was in a rotten mood. Some stuff got delivered tonight from a company that called to sell her the Century's Greatest Figurines. She said she didn't want them—so they sent them with a bill. She told them to get lost—they said "thank you for your order." I made her open the package so we could have a good laugh at the things, to cheer her up. But they had been packed really badly and were totally shattered. Seemed like a metaphor or something. Smashed little people.

After that I was in a worse mood than Mom, which is saying a lot.

Bryan was sitting there whistling, looking like he'd just won the lottery. He even *cooked*. Last thing I knew, his favorite meal was cinnamon-sugar toast. Now he's making pesto pasta surprise, or whatever he called it. Oscar was running around the kitchen in circles he was so excited about it.

Bryan also made this crunchy Italian bread with spices. The entire meal had a very distinct flavor to it: BETH.

"This is wonderful." Mom looked like she'd died and gone to heaven. A heaven with no phones and no tele-marketers. "And all vegetarian, Courtney—no dairy, even. Aren't you impressed?"

"Are you guys in a cooking class together?" I asked, my eyes narrowed at Bryan. "Is *that* how you met?"

Bryan frowned at me. "We met when you brought her over here to play Barbie about ten years ago."

"All right, you two—*no* arguing. This is a delicious meal, and I don't want it spoiled."

Then Mom's smile warbled into this look of torture because the phone rang. She grabbed the receiver and was about to yell when she said, "Oh, *hi*, Beth, well we're eating, but since I love you so much, you can talk to Bryan."

I glared at Bryan as he took the phone from Mom. I never got to talk to Dave during family meals.

I glared at Mom. What about her family-politics-school rule? Did Beth fit in there? I felt like I was underneath the family and the school rock. Smashed like an ugly figurine.

Why am I posting this e-mail in here? In case Alison ever tries to say she's never done anything mean.

Courtney:*
*[Note: not even a "dear"!]

I don't know why you're so upset. Okay, it's kind of weird, Beth and Bryan dating, and Grandma and Grandpa sleeping together. And maybe it's annoying when Dad goes on and on about Sophia. But you can't go around hating people because they're happy. Just because they found their soul mates, and you haven't found yours yet, doesn't mean you can rain on their parades. It's not fair, Courtney! We were all happy for you and Dave. What's his new girlfriend like? Have you met her?

Would you hate *me* if I told you I might be in love, too? And that's the real reason I didn't meet you for Thanksgiving? And that I've never been happier?

I'll tell you more about it at Christmas. Hang in there until then. I know you're a better person than the one who wrote me that hateful e-mail. I'm deleting it.

Love,
Alison

I think she wants to delete *me*.

We're all in trouble now. Some telemarketer told Mom he got her name from the phone company. "That's how it's done," he said. "Wake up, Mrs. Smythe." He mispronounced her name. Smith. How hard is it?

So now telemarketers are off the hit list.

MegaPhone is on it.

"They have no conscience!" she kept saying, as we sat in front of the TV, watching and eating dinner. Bryan went out with Beth; Mom and I were left to our own devices, which means pizza. About every half hour a new MegaPhone ad came on.

"We keep in touch" is their new slogan. (Their old one, "For the love of talk," got them in trouble with a bunch of religious groups, something about how they were saying they were equal to God, or the phone was equal to God.)

"They keep in touch all right," Mom kept muttering. "With our *wallets*. Stupid figurines. Stupid phone company!"

When I got to school (late and frozen, because Mom is making me ride my bike in subzero temps) (I wouldn't ask Beth for a ride because she was already giving Bryan a ride.) (What kind of relationship can they have if only one of them is old enough to drive?), Tom was waiting out front for me. He dragged me over to a corner by the entrance. This is it, I thought. He's going to make his move. Kind of bizarre at 7:45, but at least I'd know he was attracted to me. And if I could look good with ice chips on my cheeks, and some stuff coming out of my nose, well then hey.

"I have something really serious to tell you," Tom said. "I don't even know if I *should* tell you, but it affects both of us, so you need to know." He reached into his pocket. Here it comes. The standard Tom Delaney jewelry gift, I thought. I wouldn't accept it, of course. But the point was that he was finally making the offer. What's he going to tell me? I wondered. About his deep feelings for me? Yeah, right, like he has feelings. But he is cute.

He pulled out this sheet of paper. "What's that?" I asked.

"It's about the student council," he said. "We're being investigated."

"What? Is it Jennifer? Is she suing you for sexual harassment?" I'd seen this coming. As a future lawyer, I see lawsuit opportunities everywhere.

"Who?"

"*Jennifer.* You went out with her for a few months, and then she transferred to private school?"

"What?"

"Never mind," I said. She could sue him for being thoughtless and cruel, but that was about it. "What does that letter say?"

"We're being investigated. There are like, some, discrepancies. They did some sort of study of us, and they checked our books. They think we stole all this money—they think we did all these volunteer things for show to cover up the fact we were . . . embezzling or something."

"Embezzling? That's crazy," I said. "We haven't been doing anything like that." Only Tom and I had access to the checkbook. Then I looked at him. "Have we?"

"No, of course not. It's probably a clerical error or whatever. But the thing is I applied for early decision. I'm going to find out in days whether I got in or not, and I—I mean, we—have to keep this thing quiet. Keep it out of the papers, you know?" He was almost panting with nervousness.

"Like our school paper has ever broken a story. On anything?" I reminded him. "Don't sweat it."

He was so lost and desperate. I didn't know what to do. I sort of wanted to kiss him, but I also felt like telling him to grow up. This was nothing he'd go to jail over.

So the Duck informed us later that we're going to be reviewed by the Student Honor Committee (not to be confused with the National Honor Society—this group checks out *lack* of honor). And guess who's the head of the SHC? I don't know why I never noticed, maybe because I never had a problem with my HONOR before. Anyway, the committee has a member from each class, and then an "arbitrator" to lead them (they need 5 total so they can have votes). So Mr. Honor of the Year turns out to be Grant. And we have to tell him everything (except maybe the fact that I think I'm getting a crush on him) (hope he doesn't subpoena this journal).

He came to investigate and check our office. We opened the supply cabinet to show him everything we have. It was totally empty.

Mrs. Martinez is horrified.

I'm horrified.

Now we're all under this "umbrella of suspicion." Only everyone suspects me the most, because I'm the new girl. I think I'm going to be impeached.

Remember what Jennifer told me? "You have to watch everything he does." I thought she meant the back-rub thing. She was probably talking about Tom's money management, or lack thereof—and that's why she left.

"Courtney! Talk to me," Beth said. She was holding a knife to cut strawberries, so I didn't stand much of a chance. She demanded to know what was going on with the student council, and why I was still so upset about her and Bryan seeing each other.

I started out going on and on about the student council. She interrupted me—she didn't really want to hear about that at all. "Why are you unhappy for me and Bryan?" she asked.

"Because it's wrong," I said. "Because you guys have known each other for too long. Because—Beth, do I really have to *explain* this?"

"Um, yeah, you do," she said. "I'm always happy when you hook up with someone. So why can't you be happy for me?"

"You're like a sister to me. And Bryan's like a brother to me—"

"He *is* your brother," Beth said.

"I know! I know that! But see, with the transitive property, you're like a sister to him—"

"No I'm not! Don't say that. Courtney, we've hardly spent any time with him for years. We've ignored him and made fun of him—"

"And what was wrong with that?" I asked her. "Can't we just go on doing that?"

"You don't get it," she said. "Nobody gets it."

Oh my God, I thought. She's starting to talk like him!

"He's changed," she went on. "He's older now—"

"So are we!" I said. "So that still makes us two years older than him!"

"You like Grant," Beth said. "He's younger than *you*."

"What? I do not. And he's only . . ." I tried to remember when his birthday was. At most, he was two *months* younger than me. Then for some reason I got this picture of his body in my head instead of his birthday. "Just forget it!" I told Beth.

We worked in frozen silence for the rest of the afternoon. Wheatgrass Woman came in at 3:40, stared at our name tags, and said, "To tell you the truth . . . this wheatgrass sort of . . . sucks today. Are you concentrating . . . Courtney? Beth?"

"I'll make you another one," I grumbled.

"I sense hostility here," she said. "It could be the result of one of you having unsafe sex."

That's exactly it, I thought. Beth having sex with Bryan—probably not, but even if they kissed? That was definitely unsafe.

Grant is sitting by the window. WWW is hovering over him, like he's invaded her space. He's on break. She's still waiting for that bus. Please don't ask him about safe sex, I thought. And please don't ask *me* about it while *he's* here.

I went over when he first got here and sat with him for a while. He was mad because a shipment of Science Diet came in and he was the only one there to unload the truck. He was sweaty in a clean kind of way. We talked about the student council thing. "I can't really comment," he said. "Me being the arbitrator and all."

"Right. Of course," I said. "But the Duck—she's going to listen to reason, right? She won't expel us or anything."

He wouldn't answer.

Oh crap. Imagine me working here forever. Growing old(er) with WWW. Fruit and sundaes being my life. On the Banana Wheel of Fortune.

Oh my God. It *all* happened today. Still can't believe it. I got to work; Beth and I still weren't talking; then Gerry told me this would be my last day "at this location." The Boulder store is ready to open, and he wants me to be the "point person" there, work 3 afternoons a week plus Saturdays, etc. etc. etc. What? I told him I didn't want to, that I couldn't. How could someone who pretends to be into peace and harmony even suggest splitting me and Beth up? Maybe we're not talking now, but still, we have a history, we'll work it out eventually. And Boulder??? Where Dave lives??? No.

"Gerry, how can you make me work there? I can't! Absolutely not," I said.

We went back and forth. I told him I didn't have time, he told me he'd sent me to that seminar so I could do this, he explained it to me back then, he's been talking to me about it for weeks, blah blah blah. "That was before I knew about Dave and what's-her-face!" I said.

Beth was out front helping customers. We were having one of those Front Range wind blasts so no one was really rushing in. Then this kids' birthday party showed up. Gerry had completely forgotten they were coming. Ten kids. They were supposed to have a frozen yogurt cake, but it hadn't been made.

Gerry panicked. He told me and Beth to make the kids whatever they wanted—no charge. The kids were cool, but the 2 moms with them were insane. They had me make, remake, triple-make their sundaes.

I lost it when one of them complained about the pecans on her Banana Splitsville not being pecans but peanuts instead—I was so flustered I'd used the wrong bin. This woman got hysterical, and accused me of trying to give her an allergic reaction, didn't I know she could die if she ate peanuts, blah blah blah.

I told the woman *she* was nuts. Then I quit. I threw my Holstein apron on the floor and marched out, nearly knocking down Wheatgrass Woman. She looked more upset than I felt.

No way am I working in Boulder and waiting on Dave and what's-her-name. *Never!*

Home, home on the Front Range . . .
Where the deer and the antelope play
Where seldom is heard
An encouraging word
From any of my friends or ex-boyfriends or prospective
boyfriends
Or even siblings
And the skies are cloudy all day

So here I am sitting behind the counter at the new Truth or Dairy II. In Boulder. All alone.

I gave in, okay? I had to think about everything I'd be giving up. The free smoothies (like I've had one in 6 months). The endless requests for less or more ice.

Half the stuff here is still in boxes. There's a very annoying new paint smell that won't go away.

This is the opening before the Grand Opening on Saturday. This is like . . . a preview. A run-through so we can see what we've forgotten. Um . . . my guess right now would have to be: customers.

"I knew you'd come back!" Gerry cried, this giggly sound coming out of him. I'd never heard anything like it. "Oh, Courtney, I'm so proud of you. You slew the demons!"

What demons is he talking about? Dave? The fact I had to drive the Bull to Boulder and am commuting 30 miles for a $7 an hour job? The fact I hate change of any kind? Or was he talking about jealousy, hatred, dislike of other girls who date Dave . . . *Those* demons?

I'm supposed to be working with somebody named Trent. Hasn't shown yet. Don't think he will. I'm supposed to be the one who trains him. I wish he would show up so I could leave him out here by himself when Dave and Pretty Woman come in. She's probably like . . . 20 or something. Experienced. And yet still less jaded than me.

Gerry just called to see how it's going. "How come I don't hear anything in the background?" He expected blenders whirring, ice-cream scooping, nuts being chopped, I guess.

"I think you're going to need to advertise a little more," I said.

Oh hell, the door just opened and like an entire sorority is coming in. Bye for now.

LATER THAT SAME DAY

Back home, in bed. I don't know what came over me today. It was like having a high fever, the kind that gives you really weird thoughts and fears.

I got so nervous about Dave coming in, it was like I had to do something to protect myself. A shield. And I made it out of butterscotch and hot fudge. And chocolate chocolate chip ice cream.

I raced into the back room and started devouring this Turtle Shell Sundae. I *hate* butterscotch. And I hate eating around the smell of new paint.

Grant called while I was there—he'd stopped by to see me at the old store and Beth told him I was working in Boulder and gave him the number. Not that she'd use it.

"It sucks that you have to work up there," he said. "No more Canyon Boulevard." He said he'd miss seeing me around.

He was being so nice, I was afraid I was going to start crying. Or it could have been the new paint giving me an allergic reaction. Anyway, I told him I had to go because the hot butterscotch was boiling over.

"Okay, but before I go, I have to tell you that you got such a glowing recommendation from Gerry and Beth and some customers in the store. So that's going in my report—that everyone thinks you're very trustworthy."

I'm so thrilled with his dumb *report*. Can't he ask how *I* am?

Things can get worse! Who knew?

Was working in Boulder again today. Gerry doesn't seem to notice I am the only one doing horrendous commute. Beth doesn't seem to care.

So there I was. Trent not showing again. First some guy came in and asked all about the history of the store. He asked if we were kosher vegan, whether we used the same blenders for dairy and nondairy. I had to admit that we crossed the line back and forth, though I personally tried to—

Anyway, that is so not the point.

The big drama (after the woman came in and asked if we had any hot dairy drinks) (and when I said no, she asked if we had any hot smoothies) came next. Grant came in. With Dave.

My scoop slipped into the pineapple sorbet. I don't think I ever found it, I was so flustered. That has to be a health code violation.

SO ANYWAY, there they were. I guess I was glad that Dave was with Grant instead of his new girlfriend. But why was Grant in Boulder and why was he coming here and why wasn't he at work and why did he drag Dave in to see me? Was Grant the one who wanted to see me or was Dave? Was Grant only trying to be a Good Samaritan, get us to talk? Total mystery. Goes along with theory of boys needing to travel in packs, though.

But it wasn't fair because Beth wasn't there to back

me up, to be *my* pack. All of a sudden I realized how much I missed her. But there wasn't time for anything like that. I had to freak out.

I took a deep breath and put a very phony smile on my face. I asked if I could help them. Politely. Really!

"Hi, Courtney," Dave said. "Wow, your hair's getting really long."

I didn't know if that was a compliment, but since I didn't know what else to say, I said, "Thanks."

"Must be all the healthy eating you do," Dave said.

Is he trying to win me back? I wondered. By talking about my healthy hair? Or is he being sarcastic because he knows I'm not always healthy? Is he obsessed with my hair?

"Must be," I said. I turned to Grant and smiled. Even though I sort of wanted to hurl a blender at his head. What was he thinking, coming in here with Dave on a smoothie field trip? Did he have no heart?

"So how's it going?" he asked. He immediately looked down at the ice-cream tubs. Like he didn't know what chocolate chip was.

Then they ordered really easy stuff, I think they were nervous. Dave passed on the Coconut Fantasy Dream. That was like a slap in the face. He opted for the Seasonal Cranberry Splash (turkey not included).

"Couldn't get enough at Thanksgiving?" I said as I poured it into a cup. He didn't bring his refillable cup. Another slap in the face. Probably threw it out. Probably has a new refillable cup from new girlfriend.

"You know me. I love cranberry," Dave said.

No. I thought I knew you. I was wrong, thought the jaded bitter dramatic side of me.

The playful side of me said, "You do *not*."

Grant got a Banana Splitsville. Then he sat there and only ate about two bites. Don't know what's wrong with him. He kept looking over at me and smiling and then looking away like he knew he'd done the wrong thing, bringing Dave here.

Dave looked incredibly uncomfortable the whole time, too. Good. I guess it's the first time I've seen him since he started seeing what's-her-name. Well, he definitely doesn't look *happier*. Paler, maybe, and like he's got a head start on those freshman 15 everyone talks about.

I helped him along by putting extra body-building power in his smoothie. After I took their money, I felt really stupid standing there in my apron, so I went into the back for some supplies I didn't really need.

After a minute or two Dave actually came back there, following me. He said I was being very rude. Like a customer who happens to be an ex-boyfriend coming into the storeroom isn't rude? Excuse me!

"Could you just talk to us for a second?" he said. "I mean, I guess it's fine if you want to be mean to me—"

"Oh, thanks." I was so mad, I was squeezing the handful of wheatgrass so tightly that juice was almost dripping onto my shoe.

"But could you just be a little nicer to Grant?"

"Could you just *leave*?" I said.

"Courtney, come on. Why can't we be friends?" he said.

Naturally he has to use a line from a Smash Mouth song. He has no original lines!

"Oh, I'm sure we can be friends," I said. "Just not . . . maybe not for six months or so. Yeah, that sounds right. Of course your time line might be a little different—"

There was a "Moo" out front, which meant the door had opened (dumb new feature Gerry added to the new store—good thing door doesn't open as much as store back home). "Excuse me. I have customers," I said.

Dave tossed his cup into the trash. He'd hardly drunk any of his cranberry. I knew he didn't like it. Just like I knew he shouldn't have ever come in!!!

"You need to lighten up a little," he said. "Are you going for smoothie server of the year or something?"

I went out to the front and Grant was sitting there, chewing on his spoon, the Banana Splitsville totally melted in the dish. There weren't any customers. I guess someone came in, saw Grant not eating, and left.

So I walked over to Grant. "Didn't you like it? Want me to make you something else?" I offered.

"Um . . . no," he said. Then he looked up with this really pathetic look. I can't even describe it. In the meantime Dave stormed past us and went out onto the street to wait.

"Are you feeling okay?" I asked Grant.

"Sure. I just sort of wanted to . . . see where you worked. So, um, well. Here it is, right?" He seemed to come to his senses then. He got up and walked to the door. "See you later!" He waved and then went outside. Two guys were skateboarding down the sidewalk and nearly ran him down.

Grant came up *here* to see me? Sort of like when Dave drove down to the other T or D to see me? So he likes me. Grant, I mean. But when Dave drove down to Denver for a smoothie, it was to yell at me for being on student council.

I'm totally confused.

What would happen if Gerry opened a new store in Pueblo? Who would drive down then?

I hate working at this new store. Later in the afternoon, I had my back turned because Gerry bought these used blenders from a smoothie place that was going out of business, and half of them don't work, so I was using the one that did work, and someone came in and stole the stupid tip jar.

I didn't have to work today so I went to see Grant. I figured one work visit deserved another. Also I actually missed the Canyon Boulevard crowd. I never thought I'd miss that stupid strip mall, but I did. It was weird parking at that lot and not going to work myself.

Anyway, I found Grant at Pet Me. I asked him what he had in mind, bringing Dave to the store.

But I wasn't even thinking about Dave. I was worried about Grant and how he was acting and how he hadn't eaten anything. But I couldn't say that. It was like the only thing we really knew how to talk about was Dave. And we couldn't stop.

He said it wasn't his idea. He also said not to worry, that he met Dave's new girlfriend and she wasn't anything like me. (And why wouldn't that make me worry?)

"Anyway, they're on-again, off-again," he said.

"I'd rather they were off-again. Period," I said.

"Courtney, come on. It's not that bad. Anyway, I think in a way Dave did the right thing," Grant said. "Because you guys might not be happy together anymore. You've both changed a lot since the summer."

Uh-oh, I thought. He's going to call me a bitch, just like Beth! But all he did was sort of put his arm around me. Or I thought that's what he was doing. But at the same time he was also sort of adjusting this leash display rack, putting the right lengths on the right hooks.

"So, did you um . . . have a good time yesterday?" I asked.

"Oh, yeah. Definitely," Grant said. "And don't worry, I bet that store will take off soon."

"I don't want it to succeed," I said. "I want to come back and work over there." I pointed toward the original T or D.

"Yeah. That would be cool," he said. "Well, I have to go unload another truck. But I'll see you later."

"Right. Okay." I went outside and stood in the doorway for a second. Something was definitely happening between me and Grant. But we were both totally not willing to admit it.

I took a deep breath. It smelled like a mixture of stinky cages and fresh snow.

I'm writing this on the bus. It's stopping every half block and taking forever.

Mom paged me this afternoon and told me to meet her downtown. She implied it was important. I assumed it was holiday shopping, maybe she wanted to lift me out of my funk by taking me to dinner at a hot new restaurant, then we'd cruise to Larimer Square, hit some cool clothing store. But no. That isn't her style, anyway, so I don't know what I was thinking.

I met her outside the city and county building, which was all lit up for Christmas. Very festive.

Except that Mom was staging a major protest there. And she marched with a group of people from there down to MegaPhone headquarters.

"Mom. You can't yell at MegaPhone *using* a megaphone!"

"That's the beauty of it!" she said. "Fight fire with fire!"

Then she and her group started chanting: "Hell, no, we won't call! We won't use the phone at all!"

Mom was carrying a sign saying, *Hang Up On MegaPhone*! The woman next to her had one that said, *Automated Directory Assistance=Death*.

I could hear a bunch of disgruntled ex-employees ranting behind me about getting fired and replaced by computers. Then there were some current employees wearing name tags (Duh! Do you want to get fired when this is on the news?) who were complaining about how there was a cash bar at the Christmas party that year and how expensive it was.

"Mom, this is going to be on local TV," I said.

"With any luck!" she said. "Exposure is just what this cause needs right now."

"And if you stay out here all day, you're going to *die* of exposure," I argued. "You don't even have a warm coat on!"

She didn't care. About humiliation, about frostbite, about anything. Except getting the MegaPhone practices changed. I wandered around the stone steps, thinking how I could convince her to leave. I once had a friend who yelled at the phone company, and they screwed up his service, his listing, everything in retaliation. We had enough problems when MegaPhone was giving us "quality service."

That's when I saw Witchy Wheatgrass Woman, with the purple-silver magic purse. She was standing behind Mom, chanting, and holding a sign that said *Privacy Is Our Most Important Natural Resource*. Whatever that meant. She saw me and ran over to tell me how proud I should be of my mother, how she set a good example for all of us. Yes, but did you ask her if she practices safe sex? I wanted to ask her. You sure check up on me and Beth all the time about it.

Suddenly there were TV cameras swarming around Mom. "Ms. Smith! What do you have to say to the executives?"

She gave a very impressive speech. She was completely composed, like she'd been building toward this moment for years, like she had the whole thing prewritten and rehearsed. And maybe she did.

I was really proud of her. I kind of got tears in my eyes. There was a lot of dust and soot blowing around, too, so it could have been that.

Then across the way I saw the Tom show up with a bunch of his friends. I couldn't deal with them—they'd probably only make fun of Mom. The Tom isn't exactly someone you could turn to for support. So I turned to run—and I crashed right into Mr. Novotny. He was in full Broncos regalia—Broncos winter jacket, stocking cap, etc. I was surprised he had come so far into town on a game weekend. Wasn't there a playoff game happening somewhere?

"Not so fast," Mr. Novotny said when I tried to brush past him with a polite wave.

What was he going to do, *CSP on me? Wait a second, I thought. He loves those cell phone features. What's he doing here? So I asked him.

"Those features are fine—but that's through another company. How about the week when all your family's calls came to my house? That is not any way to run a business," Mr. Novotny said. "You know who they need at the helm?"

"John Elway?" I guessed, figuring this had to relate to the Broncos somehow, or his entire day would be wasted. Besides, the man is like a god around here.

"Mike Shanahan," he said. "The man can coach a Super Bowl-winning team—he can run a phone company. They ought to get his input."

"Right . . ." I said slowly. Out of the corner of my eye I saw Mom heading into the building, trying to get past Security. I ran over to her and asked what she was doing.

"I got the idea from you," she said. "I'm going to sleep on the roof until they change company policy and improve customer service."

"What policy? What service? Anyway, we weren't protesting anything!" I said.

"Same difference," she said. "You made a statement."

"But Mom, that was a school roof. This is a skyscraper! You'll be sleeping on the helicopter launchpad. You'll get crushed by executives and Flight for Life! You'll get struck by lightning!"

"It's December," she said. "How much lightning can there be?"

"This is Colorado," I said. "The weather changes really quickly, Mom."

The woman does not listen to reason.

I have to get Bryan to help me. And I have to go to Beth's house to get him.

"So. Are you going to quit being weird?" That was the first thing Beth said when she opened the door yesterday.

"No," I said. "Probably not." Then I laughed. And she said something like that was probably too much to ask for. Was I there to apologize, she asked. Actually no, I said. I'm looking for Bryan—is he here?

"I can't believe you're not going to apologize!"

"Sorry," I said. "But I'm not."

"Hm." She stood in the doorway, not budging, her Beth stance on. She should play for the Broncos. They could use her. She looked like this impenetrable offensive line.

"It wasn't so much you guys going out . . . as how you didn't tell me," I said. "I hate when people don't tell me stuff. Like Gerry, and the new store in Boulder!"

"Yeah, but that's Gerry. We're talking about us. How could you be so mean to me?" Beth asked. "I can't believe you'd write me off for going out with Bryan."

I didn't know what to say. "I'm sorry. But it's weird."

Beth shrugged. "Yeah, I kinda thought it was weird, too. I guess that's why I couldn't tell you. So come in, and I'll get Bryan. What's going on?"

I told her about Mom and her crusade for 5-cent Saturdays. Bryan was lying on the sofa in the basement, reading. Beth grabbed her coat and told Bryan to get his and we were out of there.

By the time we got back downtown, Mom was nowhere to be found. I thought maybe they were holding her in the MegaPhone headquarters. Subjecting her to really loud dial tones.

Turned out she gave up and came home. "They agreed to a meeting," she said. "With me and any other consumers who have complaints. I hope they have a big enough building."

"They could use Mile High Stadium," I said. It seats about 80,000.

We laughed.

Then Mom picked up the phone to call Dad and finalize the Christmas plan. And there was no dial tone.

Beth called me at the T or D II, since our phone at home is still not working. Mom is considering legal action, but then, when isn't she? I think we're switching to some tiny telephone company that has zero features and isn't even legal yet. Whatever. She has her meeting at MegaPhone on December 30. I think they gave her that date because everyone's out of town on vacation and nobody else will show for the meeting.

"Listen, Courtney—I have a plan. We're getting you out of that Boulder store," Beth said.

I asked her how. She made it sound like a top-secret plan, as if we were going to strike in the middle of the night. Mercenaries. Smoothie mercenaries. Watch your back and also your nonfat raspberry sherbet.

"We've worked at the place for two years," she said. "We've shown Gerry nothing but loyalty. We've invented drinks. We could have gone and worked for any other smoothie place in town. But did we? No. And we can tell him we were even like recruited by these other places," Beth said. "They *begged* us to work for them, but we said no, even though they pay 75 cents more per hour."

"Hey, wait a second," I said. "So then . . . why aren't we working there instead?"

Hm. We both thought about it for a second.

"Maybe we should," Beth said. "But we stay at T or D because we like working together, and we like guaranteeing freedom of frozen choices, and um . . . we sort of

226

like Gerry. Because we like his nonstandard approach to life."

"And we like banana splits," I added.

"But if he wants us to stick around, he has to let us work together, at the Canyon Boulevard location, and this is like nonnegotiable."

Girl power!

Then Beth asked me something else. "Can you work for me Tuesday night so Bryan and I can go to a movie? We want to celebrate the last day of school before vacation."

It was like swallowing wheatgrass juice on an empty stomach with no water back. But I can handle that. And I could handle this, I told myself. Just . . . not all that well.

"Sure," I said.

Beth and I gave Gerry the ultimatum. He said he'd *think* about it! What? How insulting is that.

So I quit again. It's not so hard, the second time around.

Beth quit, too. Gerry pretty much looked shocked.

We figure we'll have a much better vacation. Also, now I don't have to cover for her tomorrow night. "Want to go to the movies with me and Bryan?" she asked.

"Um . . . no, that's okay. I have plans," I said. I kept it vague. She didn't believe me anyway, so there was no point wasting valuable time coming up with a story.

One more day of school before Christmas break. We're meeting tomorrow to talk about the New Year's party. I don't know what's going on with the investigation—I guess it's "ongoing."

Random Nosebleed is playing at the party. My idea. They came up with their name after two of the guys got nosebleeds on stage, out of nowhere.

Well, okay, probably it was because the air is drier than toast out here in the winter. Ick. I got one at work once. Blood fell into the smoothie I was making.

Gag. Just thinking about watching the drops fall into the blender could make me puke now. I'll have to finish this later. I feel really ill.

Grant and I had lunch today. He asked how I was doing (fine, considering I had no job), whether I was going to the big Lebeau Christmas party tomorrow night (yes), and what I had planned for tonight.

I felt this utter panic. He wasn't asking me to lunch anymore. He was asking me to do stuff outside of school. He was asking for a date. Tonight! And I couldn't go. I liked him too much.

"Nothing," I said. "I mean—because I have to work for Beth."

Then he asked if I wanted to go skiing over Christmas vacation.

"I can't," I said. "We're not supposed to fraternize, right? You're still investigating us."

"We'll be on vacation," Grant said. "I won't be thinking about your case. It should be wrapped up by then anyway."

"Oh. Really?"

"Sure. So do you want to go?"

"Well, um, I don't ski much," I said. "It's bad for the environment."

"Snow is bad for the environment?"

"Driving up to the mountains is. There's so much traffic and then you have to go over those passes, and—"

"I'll drive. We could take the Ski Train," Grant suggested.

He wouldn't stop.

"I actually haven't skied in a really long time," I said. "I'm really bad, so . . . I'm sure I'd just hold you back." I smiled uneasily. I knew from ski trips with Dave and his friends that Grant was the best snowboarder of all of them. "And anyway, I'll probably have to work, so . . ."

Right then there was this overhead page. "Courtney Smith, please report to the principal's office. Immediately."

"Uh-oh," I said. "I must be in big trouble—the Duck wants to see me."

"Yeah. You must be," Grant said. He was practically glowering at me. What did I do? Just because I didn't want to go skiing—

But I did want to go skiing. But I can't! I can't like Grant. It won't work out.

The Duck asked if I'd seen Tom that day. I hadn't. Then she said that our final meeting, our New Year's party—everything—is off. There will be no Random Nosebleed or even a planned nosebleed.

Six checks we used to pay for the party bounced. The student council fund is completely empty. We have no money left!

Jane and Beth and I met at 10:00 to go Christmas shopping and to buy outfits for upcoming parties like the big one at the Lebeau Mansion tonight. We spent about three hours cruising around the mall—didn't find anything.

"The mall is so bad compared to Discount Duds," Jane said as she trotted around in somebody else's used crinkled black boots. Her outfit was vintage from head to toe. And she was wearing this plastic watch she got for free from the Complete gas station.

She kind of dresses like she's in a band now, and maybe she should be. It's weird, though, hearing Jane say she hates the mall. Talk about a turnaround. Her parents are horrified.

Then we went to a department store cafe where Jane could charge lunch to her parents' plastic, just to let them know she hasn't changed *that* much. I finally told them what had happened with Grant. They nearly fell off their chairs.

"So Grant asked you out. Wow. I don't think Grant's asked out anyone in like . . . a year," Jane said. She adjusted her bubble-gum color plastic glasses. *She* can wear them. She can wear anything. "Not since Beth broke his heart."

"I didn't break his heart," Beth said. "I wounded him slightly. I didn't know he was going to be so sensitive about it."

231

I knew Beth's angle on the whole thing. I wanted to know Jane's. "How do you know he hasn't gone out with anyone else?" I asked.

"It's obvious." She shrugged. "I thought he was still pining for Beth, but obviously he's been saving himself for you. And then you go and say *no*. Why?"

"Because. I told you, I'm not seeing anyone this year."

"Why? Because of Dave?" Jane asked. "Who you haven't talked to in a really long time and who has a girl-friend and who you're basically completely over now?"

"You're letting Dave ruin your senior year!" Beth said.

"*Our* senior year," Jane said. "This affects all of us. At first I thought your no-dating pledge was sort of cute. Now I think it's ridiculous. Remember me when I was so shortsighted that I wouldn't even shop anywhere but at the mall? I gave that up. You can give up not dating."

"And I gave up running from love," Beth said. "Having meaningless relationships instead of a real con-nection with someone. Plus smoking. And now I'm giving up gum. So if we can do all that, I think you can consider going *skiing* with *Grant*."

"You guys!" I said. I was drowning in a shower of crit-icism. "We're not talking about giving up matching hand-bags and—and—Marlboro Ultra Lights. And as far as this running-from-love bit, we don't *all* have to date—"

"Just to date? No, of course not," Beth said. "But when you find someone—"

"Who says I've found someone?"

"You just did! It's Grant, and you know it." Beth's

eyebrow was twitching. Either she's been watching too much TV and has eyestrain or she was getting extremely annoyed with me. "But you're so caught up in sticking to some plan, like you've ever stuck to any of your plans!"

"What? What are you saying?"

All the lady shoppers were staring at us.

"Quit making pledges you can't keep," Beth said. "About campaigns, about food, about boys—about everything!" Then she stood up, tossed her linen napkin onto the table, and went to the bathroom. Too bad she was wearing black pants, because she had a ton of lint on her pants now and looked sort of silly, and everyone was still staring at us.

I pulled my chair closer to the table and sipped my lemon water. "I keep pledges," I told Jane. "I'm *good* at pledges. Like the Pledge of Allegiance. In second grade I was chosen to say it on Parents' Day."

"We're not talking about the *flag*," Jane said. "We're talking about your life."

"My life is fine," I said.

The way I see it, I'm the only one with any integrity. I'm the only one who's kept up her standards. Why does everyone *have* to date? I mean, what is so wrong with being by yourself once in a while, or all the time even?

Except for the fact that it's sort of boring, and I would so like to see Grant on a snowboard.

REALLYREALLY LATE OR EARLY ON THE 24TH

This is Courney's jrnl. My writing. I'm drunk. Me, Alson, the oldes mos responsbl one.

Is it my fault the punch at the Lebeaus' was spiked? Mr. Lebeau said it was Santa's elfs. Elves. Whatever. I know who didit.

Mr. Lebeau wants to fix me up with his son Mark. Like I'd like Mark. I'm in love with Jessie. And nobody here knows anything about it.

Mom is outside arguing with a man on a telfon pole. Don't knowhy. Courtney do you?

yes, definitely, whatever you say Alison
I love Dave
tom doesn't have a thing for me, but I kissed him anyway
I hate Mrs. Malloy's cookies
I hate Martha Stewart
where is lake superior?

In Canada, stupid.
Happy Holidays,
love,
alison

Complete nightmare. I can hardly write, my hand is so shaky. "You're hungover!" Alison cried, jumping on my bed. "Isn't it cool?"

"*No*," I said, before running to the bathroom to hurl.

Then the doorbell rang. At the same time, I heard this teensy tiny baby crying. Could it be any louder?

Alison and I crawled downstairs. It's *Dad*. And Sophia. And Sophia's kid, Angelina. And Angelina's new baby. They just drove up from Phoenix.

I guess I knew Dad is now a granddad (which means this baby's *great*-grandparents are having Viagra-induced sex and that's totally disturbing) (or wait, that's the other side of the family—am I still drunk?), but it still seems very bizarre. He was so excited to see us. He gave me a huge hug. And I'm really glad he's here, don't get me wrong. But when he hugged me I knew right away I was going to hurl again. But he wouldn't let go, and Alison was in on it, too, of course *she* doesn't have a throbbing headache and the seasick feeling I got when I went rafting on my 14th birthday and got my period in the middle of the Arkansas and had to turn the full-day rafting trip into a half day. I wanted to put myself into a dry bag.

Anyway, Mom was out shopping for food, so Sophia came running after me when I sprinted to the bathroom. I told her to go away—that Alison could take care of me. But Alison was busy talking to Angelina and playing with the baby. Whatever her name is. So I spent some quality time with the dry heaves. Now I'm lying on my bed. Mom will be home soon, and then all hell will break loose.

I have to hand it to her, actually. The woman has nerves of steel, inviting Dad and his new family to her house. I can't even handle seeing Dave at a party.

Speaking of which, I still have to write down what happened at the Lebeau Mansion.

Alison is so different! She confessed to me that *she* was the one who spiked the punch. Very impressive. As long as we were all walking to the party, I guess it's okay. She kept talking about some guy named Jesse. She was so lit she even spelled his name wrong in here.

What a night. I still can't get over it. I don't know what to do.

Everyone was there. I mean, the place was so crowded, full of everyone I know from school and their parents. Alison and I went together, sort of late. She immediately headed for the punch bowl. That skinny Mark Lebeau made a beeline for *me*. So I looked around and saw Beth and Jane. They were talking to Grant!

I kind of panicked. I hadn't *seen* Grant since turning him down a few days ago. And Jane and Beth were probably telling him to ask me out again, encouraging him to like wear me down. The fact he was even talking to Beth again was weird. I wanted to go home. But the crowd pushed me forward, a surge for the fruitcake and eggnog table.

I ended up right in front of them. They were in the middle of telling him how I've decided to be a nun this year. But the way they said it made it sound incredibly stupid instead of brilliant.

"Look, here comes Sister Courtney," they teased me.

"Shut up," I said, not meeting Grant's eyes.

"You look incredible—for a nun," Jane said. "Love that green velveteen. Totally matches your eyes."

"Um, thanks," I said. Don't draw attention to me! I thought. We want Grant to think I'm unattractive, so he can move on, forget about me, quit asking me out.

Because it's going to mess everything up for me if he keeps asking, because I don't know how many no's I have in reserve.

I glanced at him. He looked really cute, he had a tie on and everything. He was looking around the room, not at me. Perfect, I thought. Then he said, "So, Courtney. Do you want to get some punch?"

"Ah, well, ah," I stammered. Beth grabbed my arm and shoved me toward Grant. It was like we were in junior high again. "Sure."

So we went over to the punch bowl. Alison was there, which was great. We hung out with her, laughing, and she kept filling our glasses and we kept drinking punch—only because it was so crowded and hot in there, not because I knew it was spiked, honestly. When we thought about moving, we couldn't, because of the crowd. So there I was, trapped with Grant.

Mom came over to get punch and we laughed with her. Grant's parents came over, and I met them (have no idea what their names are now). Off in the distance I could see Bryan and Beth, cuddling on a sofa by the fire. "They're so cute!" I said to Alison. Getting a little tipsy, so I loved everyone.

"I'm so glad Bryan found someone," Alison said.

Then I looked over at Grant. Was he still pining for Beth? Did seeing her with my little brother give him a jealous fit?

"Your brother's a really good runner," he said.

"Oh, yeah," I said. "He's *so* good."

Then I had to find the bathroom, so Alison went with me. We were wandering around the party, and I was feeling a bit dizzy. The Tom waved to me from across the dining room and I was just about to stop and say hello when I saw Dave come around the corner. PANIC!

I hadn't seen him since that awkward day in Boulder when he yelled at me. I hadn't talked to him since then, either. But I knew one thing. I was *not* about to let him see me being Sister Courtney.

I'll show him, I thought. He's not the only one who can move on and grow!

I grabbed a hunk of mistletoe and shoved the Tom under it. Then I started kissing him.

Oh no, I realized. I'm kissing a boy. I'm kissing THE TOM. This is wrong! No boys no boys no boys! This alarm went off in my drunken head.

I shoved Tom away and he knocked the Sangria bowl onto the floor, taking three plates of Mrs. Malloy's special Christmas spritzes with it. They landed cookie-side up, but then the sangria drowned them. She got so mad! But then she went out to her Volvo and brought in 3 more trays. She's like this traveling Martha Stewart. I'd like to see them in a bakeoff.

So then Tom is looking at me all weird. Well, sure, I made a pass, and that was pretty much a shock to both of us. Grant is there, too, and he looks completely upset.

"How could you *do* that?" he asks.

And me, drunken girl, says, "I'm sorry, but they're only cookies, she can make more."

Then Grant looked furious.

And Dave is looking at me like I've just taken off my shirt and am dancing topless on the buffet table. Like he's appalled and intrigued, all at the same time.

And then this woman comes around the corner, reaching for Dave's arm like he tried to ditch her but she isn't going to let him. She's about six feet tall, like him, with blond hair and this holiday ensemble that's a little too coordinated.

Seeing them together made me want to kiss Grant again—I mean Tom—but he was kind of covered in sangria. So instead I ran outside, and started sprinting down the street for home.

"Courtney!" Tom came out after me. "Courtney, wait!"

I turned around to wave at him, and my legs went out from under me. I fell right on my butt, in the middle of the street. That's where I was sitting when Dave ran outside, too.

They both started to help me up, like chivalry wasn't

dead, like they were competing to see who could help me up faster, with which arm. I looked back at the house, wondering if Grant was going to come after me.

Instead Alison came running out a second later. "I'll drag her home," she said, taking my hands from both of them. "She's *my* sister." Her voice was this slurry mess, it came out more like "shemssis."

Dave gave me this sort of forlorn look as he let go of me. Then Tom did the same thing. Like maybe I'm a lost cause. Grant was nowhere in sight.

Alison and I skidded the entire five blocks home.

LATER THAT SAME DAY

I'm upstairs after spending half an hour sitting with Angelina in the living room. Totally awkward. Not because we're stepsisters now, but because we don't have anything in common. Not even close.

She was sitting there, nursing her baby.

I was sitting there, nursing my Surge.

Still can't believe I made out with the Tom in front of a crowd. Grant was so mad at me! He probably won't talk to me again.

There's more!

Christmas Eve. Sitting in front of the fire, waiting for dinner. Hangover fading. Mom and Sophia are cooking dinner together, so civilized you can't believe it.

Here's the setup for tonight (does it get more complicated than this?):

Dad, Sophia, Angelina, Babyrina

Mom, Alison

Grandma and Grandpa Callahan (just back from their second honeymoon in Hawaii, looking very tan and skin-cancerous) (and SATISFIED)

Bryan, Beth (just back from their honeymoon at the Park Meadows Mall)

Sorry, that was catty.

I think I've left someone out. Oh, right. *Me.*

And Oscar, who with any luck will lie under the table and not across Babyrina.

Dave called earlier to say Merry Christmas. I wished him one, too.

Tom has called three times today. I don't know if I can talk to him yet. My hangover went away, but then the memories came back. Me grabbing him. And me kissing him.

Screw the rules. They don't apply at Christmas parties. Right?

We heard a clatter of footsteps during our dinner—not on the rooftop, on the sidewalk. Grandpa started to recite the Christmas story about creatures not stirring and mice and reindeer, but then the doorbell rang. I heard my mother say, "Well, hello there, Tom!"

Tom? I thought. Oh no, what is he doing here? I did not want to see him. What if he expected me to kiss him again?

"I just need to talk to Courtney," he said when Mom brought him into the dining room.

"Well, that's fine, but why don't you join us for supper?" Mom got an extra plate and some silverware and Bryan pulled up a chair. Beth shot me this look, like: *You realize what you've gotten yourself into. Don't you?*

"Who *are* you?" my father asked.

"This is Tom," I said. "Tom Delaney. The president of the student council."

Someone kicked me under the table, then Tom whispered, "Not anymore."

"He's the boy who rescued us on the way to Ogallala," my mother explained. She handed him a giant plate of food. "When Courtney drove us off the road."

"Mom! I didn't try to," I said. When is she going to stop bringing that up???

"Does he have to eat every holiday meal with us?" Bryan mumbled to me.

Meanwhile, Tom was making himself at home. I guess

whatever he needed to talk to me about could wait. Which was fine.

"Can you pass the bread?" Tom asked Grandma. "And the relish plate, if you don't mind. And the salt and pepper, Beth?"

"Where's my silver lighter? I want my lighter," my grandfather demanded, staring at him.

"I don't have it," Tom said, calmly clearing off the relish plate onto his plate with a knife. "I did have it, but then I sold it." He dug into his chicken cordon bleu.

"What?" I thought my grandfather was going to have a stroke. I was pretty appalled, myself.

Grandma kept patting his knee and urging him to have another bite of the excellent mashed potatoes. "There's chicken broth in there, Stanley, try it," she urged.

My grandfather ate nothing. Tom cleaned his plate.

I had some green beans and spent a lot of time looking around at everyone, hoping they didn't hate me because Tom was here. After a while it was too much to take, so when Mom made a break for the kitchen and the pies, I asked Tom to come into the den with me.

"So what's the big emergency?" I said.

He paced around for a minute and then he dropped onto the sofa, facedown, and mumbled something into the pillows.

"What did you say?" I asked.

A muffled voice came out from the chenille. "I took all the student council money."

"What?" I cried, yanking the pillow out from under

him. He sat up and looked at me like he was about to cry.

"I spent it all, Court. On myself. And it's wrong, I know it's wrong, I kept trying to stop, but I couldn't. I have a problem, I need help!" Then he went on and on about how he was never going to get into college now, and his life was over. "Courtney! You've got to help me, I'm going down in flames!" blah blah blah.

The door opened and Angelina came in with a crying Bellarina and started to feed her. We ignored her.

"Tom, you were only in charge for a few months," I said. "How did you manage to blow all that money—"

"I act fast, okay? In all things. It's a character trait. I bought stuff. Gifts. That sleeping bag—"

"You bought a dumb extralarge sleeping bag with everyone else's money?" I cried.

"Hey, you slept in it, too," Tom said. "And if you don't help me get out of this, I can tell everyone you were an accomplice—"

"I'll help you, I'll help you. So, okay, let me get this straight," I said. "In addition to being a sex addict, you're a kleptomaniac, a thief—"

"Hey! *You* liked me. *You* kissed me," he said.

"Under duress!" I said.

"Oh, right. Sure," he said. "It was all about Dave, wasn't it?"

I ignored him and told him I was sure he could make an arrangement to pay the money back. I'd negotiate on his behalf. He'd be my first client. (Figures. Most clients are reprehensible and guilty.) He'd probably have to resign as president. I could take over for him, and maybe we'd keep this out of the papers—

Then I realized that as I was talking, all he was doing was staring at Angelina, who was sitting on the couch, breast-feeding Babyrina. His mouth was wide-open—he was nearly drooling as much as Babyrina.

I just couldn't believe him! I was getting completely outraged on her behalf. Then I realized they had made eye contact, and she was like . . . enjoying this. As much as he was.

I had to get out of there right away. I went back to the dinner table and smiled uneasily at everyone. "Sorry about that."

"You're not . . . dating that young man, are you?" Grandma asked.

"Oh, no," I said. "Not at all." I chewed a bite of chicken cordon bleu and thought for a second. Not about the fact that what I was eating went against everything I believed in. Not about the fact I'd been really dumb to even spend five seconds wishing I were with Tom and wanting him to notice me. Not even about the fact that I had seen skis under the Christmas tree and they were probably for me and why had I told Grant I couldn't go and was it too late to say yes.

But what I kept thinking was: If Tom hooks up with Angelina . . . if he marries Angelina, and she's my stepsister, then what would he be to me? (Besides an ex-student-council-president.) My second stepbrother-in-law once kissed and twice removed?

Merry Christmas, Part II. Fa la la la! Got exactly what I wanted from Santa: a surprise. (Not the skis, which are way cool and which Dad and Sophia got for me.) (And did I mention Bryan, Alison, and I pooled together and got Mom a cell phone that comes with no features at all except an unlisted number?)

This friend of Alison's came tonight. She drove all the way from California, through the night, straight through.

Though maybe that isn't the best way to say it. Straight through. Because I realized as soon as she came in the door and hugged Alison that *this* was the Jessie Alison was in love with. A *girl*! Not a Jesse at all.

How dumb of me not to get it before this! Can this family not clue me in once in a while? Must people hit me over the head to tell me who they're dating?

They're in this band together: Alison plays cello, Jessie sings—they played a tape for me of them. Jessie sort of sounds like Sarah McLachlan. (Wonder if they'll play at our party—for free.) She has long blond hair and is very short and petite and has six piercings in one ear.

Alison is into girls. That's why she never had a boyfriend. She doesn't like boys.

Talk about a boy-free zone. My own sister, out of the closet, and I didn't even know she was in it. Am I dense or what?

"Don't feel bad," she said. "I didn't tell anyone in the family yet—nobody knows."

"But Mom—Dad—"

"I'll tell them," she said. "Just not on this trip. I figure I can wait until the timing's better, and we have more time to talk."

"More time? You mean, you *want* more time to talk to them about it?" I said. "Because I can't stand talking with Mom and Dad about who I like and all that."

"Courtney, I was talking about five minutes, that's all," Alison said.

We both cracked up laughing. Then all of a sudden we hugged again and we were both almost bawling. I realized how much I love her and what a jerk I've been lately.

"And don't hate guys because of Dave or because of me or Dad or anything. Just do what you want to!" she told me.

It was like this Power Bar speech.

Suddenly I knew exactly what to do.

I think.

I went to find Grant to tell him about Tom confessing the day before, how the generous holiday brought out the truth in him. I wanted to ask him what we could do about still holding the New Year's party. And also to say I got skis for Christmas and did his offer still stand of going skiing together.

Day after Christmas: biggest shopping day of the year. Even Pet Me was packed. People using gift certificates for collars and hairball remedies. So I thought I'd wait for a lull. I thought I'd stand in the parking lot for a couple of hours, actually. The whole idea of seeing Grant petrified me.

I walked over to Truth or Dairy and peeked in. Gerry was behind the counter, and he had a line. I felt kind of bad for him, he was definitely flustered.

Back at Pet Me I found Grant stocking shelves. "Hey," I said. "How are you?"

He glanced at me. Briefly.

"I came by for a couple of things," I said.

He pointed across the store. "Oscar's food is over there."

I laughed. "No, not that. I mean, I had some things I wanted to tell you. And ask you." My voice was starting to sound weird and thin and shaky. "First off, Tom confessed to taking all the money. And I called Mrs. Martinez and left a message about how he'll resign and how the Duck—with your guys' input, of course—can decide on his punishment. Maybe he can pay it all back eventually." I looked around the crowded store. "Hey, are you guys hiring? Maybe he could work here."

Grant just kept shelving cans of cat food. Chicken mushroom flavor. He wouldn't even look at me.

"So I don't know if I told you, but Beth and I quit at Truth or Dairy," I said. "So I won't get to see you as much anymore, which is too bad."

He didn't blink. "I know you quit. I found out when I decided to drop by and visit you Tuesday night. You said you couldn't go out with me because you had to work? And you weren't there. And Gerry told me you *quit* on Monday."

Turns out Grant is really mad at me for lying to him not once but many times.

He said I lied to him about not knowing how to ski well. (He saw me ski once, when we all went together.)

He said I lied to him about Thanksgiving in Nebraska and how Tom was there.

He said I was a total hypocrite; I wouldn't go out with him, I said I wouldn't go out with anyone. But here I was, making the moves on Tom, who is only the worst living example of the species, a liar, a cheater, a philanderer.

A what?

"But see . . . I'm not interested in Tom, and that's why I kissed him. And I did it because I panicked when I saw Dave, so I had to kiss someone, so there was Tom, and—" Saying it out loud was so embarrassing. It made no sense. "So anyway, I don't care what they think."

"Really? It doesn't seem that way to me," Grant said, still sticking price tags on top of cans.

The thing is, the kiss meant nothing to me. Or Tom. Or even Dave, who could see it was false. But I guess it meant something to Grant. I've never seen him look mean before. It was awful!

"Grant, come on. I was sort of tipsy that night, remember?"

"Of course I remember. I was *with* you, remember? And I thought we were sort of hanging out together," Grant said. "I thought we were having fun. But as usual I guess I was wrong, and you didn't mean anything you did or said that night. Just, you know, like a *guy* would do."

Whoa. Talk about harsh!

I couldn't think of what to say. This was it. I had to tell him that I was wrong and that I did like him and that I was getting too wrapped up in a dumb self-imposed regulation which didn't take into account the fact I'd get to know someone like Grant this year, just like my nondairy rule didn't take into account the fact that Ben and Jerry would come up with new irresistible flavors every year.

"Excuse me, young man, but is anybody else working here?" a man in a plaid coat asked. "Because I need some help picking out the right cat litter. Now, I've got the clumping kind at home, but it gets tracked all over the house and it's like living at the beach, so I thought—oh, I'm sorry. Are you still helping her?"

Grant turned to me. "Am I?"

I couldn't even answer him. I couldn't speak. All I knew was that I'd ruined everything. "No," I mumbled.

Then I tried to run out of Pet Me, but the place was so crowded I couldn't get through to the exit. I tried to hurdle a scratching post and nearly fell into a fish tank. People were laughing at me. I was crying.

Spent all last night mulling over all the things I've done wrong lately.

Woke up with a brilliant idea today. We can have a school fund-raiser at the Canyon Boulevard strip mall, while everyone's out spending Christmas bucks and prone to blowing money on nothing. We could coordinate the effort, me and Beth and Grant and whoever else can help—Jane can stand on the sidewalk looking like she does and cars will pull in. It's too cold for a car wash; people's locks will freeze. But we can offer free smoothies with every pet grooming/dog wash/etc. Not full-size smoothies; maybe half-size. We can offer photos of groomed pets with ribbons, etc.

Two problems with this plan:

(1) Beth and I no longer work at Truth or Dairy.

(2) Our Pet Me connection, Grant, no longer speaks to me.

I have to try anyway, or my entire fall will be a waste.

Yes! I went back to Truth or Dairy, found Gerry. He was miserable and about to call me and Beth to ask us to come back. I said we could, but I made the school fund-raiser part of the negotiation, convinced him what good publicity we'd get, and told him it was time for him to give back to all the students who worked so hard for him. He caved. Then we set my work schedule for next week.

"Courtney, I hope you come back here feeling refreshed," he said. "Ready to throw yourself back into the job with the same enthusiasm you're showing for this school event."

"Oh, I will," I said. "And about me not working in Boulder and all that . . . no hard feelings, right?"

"Right," Gerry agreed. "Just . . . hard ice cream. And a real soft spot right here—" He meant to pat his heart, but he hit his stomach— "for you and Beth. You have done a lot for T or D, and the regulars have been asking for you. Promise me you'll stay until you graduate!"

So I did.

Then I ran over to find Grant again. He wasn't working, but I talked to the manager about my idea. He said he'd offer the grooming services for half price and the other half could go to Bugling Elk. He said to work out the details with Grant and then call him. I told him the event has to be, like, tomorrow. Or the 30th at the latest. Grant might not return my call by then. He said he'd call Grant now and let him know I'd be calling to follow up later. "Your mother's been buying dog food here for years. It's the least I can do," he said.

I called Beth, Jane, then rest of student council. That was easy. Talked with Mrs. Martinez, and she said the principal was willing to make a deal where Tom did hours and hours of community service, *plus* he had to write a letter to the school newspaper admitting his guilt and apologizing, *plus* he had to pay back all the money, and then *maybe* she wouldn't let the colleges he applied to know about it. It would go on his record, though. It sounded like Tom was going to be awfully busy for the rest of the year.

Grant finally called me at the end of the day. I told him about the fund-raiser idea and he said he thought it was cool, that he'd think about helping. "But you're like the cornerstone of this whole thing," I said. "I can't do it without you!"

"Oh. Really?" He sounded more interested after that.

"You and I have to do it together—I mean, we'll have help, but you need to be there," I said.

"Why?" he said.

"Because you're *honorable*. And nobody's going to hand over any money to me—I've been tainted," I said.

He laughed, and we got into the particulars. Like how it's supposed to be really cold tomorrow, "polar bear weather" they said on the news.

Then I went out on a major iceberg. I asked if he wanted to go to the zoo with me and actually *see* the polar bears. "Since it's polar bear weather, they'll be out playing and swimming. We can see all the other animals, too.

255

We can walk around and talk about the fund-raiser."
While I waited for his answer I pulled a tassel off the end
of the couch. Oops.

"No, I'd better not," he finally said. "It might be a
date or something, and you'd hate that. Let's just do the
fund-raiser. I'll see you tomorrow."

He's still mad. Still not forgiving me.

Damn.

Event is tomorrow. One pet who won't be groomed is Oscar. He's gone again. He was outside playing in the new snow and Mr. Novotny came roaring out of the garage with his snowblower and Oscar got so freaked out he ran away.

He went down the snowy street like he was in *Call of the Wild* and he was heading for the mountains and wasn't coming back. Only he should, like White Fang. Only White Fang would eat Oscar in about two seconds.

Oscar won't make it in the wild. He won't even make it at someone else's house, because he needs his medication. And I found his collar on the street. So nobody will see the tag that says that. They'll know when Oscar has a grand mal seizure that something is up.

I was posting signs for MISSING—SICK DOG when Grant drove up beside me. "Can I help?" he said.

"Are you following me again?" I asked. Trying to make a joke. Failing.

"Your coat's kind of bright. Couldn't help seeing you," he said. Like I was a dog myself—my "coat?"

Then I looked down and realized I had this bright pink jacket of Mom's on. I'd run out the door in such a hurry, I'd grabbed it. Me. In bright pink. In broad daylight. No wonder Grant saw me.

"We'll find him. We will," Grant said. "Did you check the pasta factory yet?"

I nodded. "The brewery, the supermarket warehouses—

257

everything bright and flashy I could think of. Even the X-rated theaters on Colfax."

"I didn't know Oscar was into that," Grant said.

"It's the flashing lights, not the porn!" I said. Then I realized Grant was only joking.

He was in a good mood again. He didn't hate me. (Wherever you are? Thanks, Oscar.) He's completely in on the Smoothie Out Your Pet plan for tomorrow. Have to work on the slogan, though.

Have to find Oscar.

Other possible slogans:

"Truth or Science Diet"

"Clean Up Your Pet and Your Diet"

"Fluffy and Smoothie—Together Again!"

Temperature dropped about twenty degrees today. Not a good sign for (a) Oscar's survival, (b) our class fundraiser. If Random Nosebleed doesn't get their full money, they won't play. Very hard-nosed about it considering they are prone to unpredictable nasal bleeding.

We still need to buy everything else for the party—with cash, because no one will take our checks now.

Everyone really pitched in: Jane getting people to bring in their dogs and cats, two guys giving complimentary flea dips to all pets, Beth and me making smoothies, Grant and this guy Larry grooming them—the dogs, I mean, not the smoothies. It was fun. We didn't even get any dog hair in anyone's drink or sundae.

But at the end of the day, when I looked at the proceeds, I could tell we wouldn't be able to pull it off. Our New Year's party was dead in the water. Or frozen in the blender, more accurately.

"We don't have nearly enough money here. You know what I need to get this party off the ground?" I said. "A grant."

Beth started laughing. "You know what you just said?"

"What?"

"You need *a Grant. Him!*" Beth pointed at Grant, who was busy trimming a Portuguese water dog with black hair.

"Quiet," I said. But it was true.

259

I'd been worried about Mom all day, how her meeting went with MegaPhone. When I got home, she wasn't there. She came in about an hour later, completely happy. She hadn't been there at all. She'd been shopping— buying cell phones for all of us. The meeting was called off because the level of consumer complaints was so high, the state has created a special commission to investigate.

MegaPhone offered to give every consumer a $10 credit for the inconveniences. Governor said no, that wouldn't even begin to cover it. He turned it over to the consumer attorney general, or someone like that.

Ha! See how *you* like being under the umbrella of suspicion.

Mom and I spent most of the night calling each other on our new cell phone numbers from different rooms of the house. Cracking up.

I only got Mr. Novotny's house once when I tried to call Mom. I didn't tell her about it.

An absolutely incredible thing just happened! Grandma and Grandpa Callahan greeted me at breakfast with a huge surprise.

"We don't want your party to be canceled." They handed me a check for a lot of money, made out to the student council.

"Especially not because of that Tom person," Grandma said. "He ought to be arrested, that's what they should do with him."

"I want my lighter," Grandpa said. "But if I can't have that, I want you kids to have fun tonight."

My eyes widened as I stared at the check. "But—but—this is too much money," I said. "Don't you need this?" For your Viagra prescription? I thought.

They said they wanted to be involved in my life and do something for the community. And they could see how hard I was working, and how I could make a difference, how everyone needed to have a good time now and then. I had to promise them a hundred times that none of the money would go toward alcohol or drugs.

Having sexually satisfied grandparents is not a bad thing at all!

Happy New Year!

Sad, isn't it? The beginning for some is the end for many. Like this sketchbook. Only 5 pages left and I have to cram in everything that happened and then put you in a time capsule so someone can find you in 50 years. Like they'd want to.

Better make it 100 years—that way I won't be around when it's opened. Spare me the pain and humiliation. Decompose or something, will you?

Well, the party went great. Mrs. Martinez made an announcement about everything that had happened with student council, and she said how I'd managed to turn lemons into lemonade and the next thing I knew she had appointed me interim president, meaning I'll probably get to keep the job and run student council for the rest of the year. Everyone cheered. It was unbelievable.

I knew Tom was at the party somewhere, hiding in a coat room or a locker or something. He'd come out when Mrs. Martinez wasn't around to yell at him. I just didn't want to see him.

Random Nosebleed was awesome. Everyone danced. Jane, Beth, and I danced together, like usual. Bryan sprained his ankle running the other day, so he was out of commission. Which was cool, not that I want him to be hurt, but it was fun to just be the three of us.

"You really made this happen," Jane said.

"The lead singer keeps checking you out," I told her.

"He's cute," she said. "I want his leather jacket."

"Okay . . ." I said. It was this scuffed-up thing that looked like it had been run over by a truck and then singed with cigarette burns.

When the clock struck midnight the band threw all these noseplugs and little packets of Kleenex into the crowd—that's their trademark. Jane, Beth, and I hugged each other, and then the crowd broke up.

When I was leaving, Grant stopped me. I'd been avoiding him all night. I couldn't ask him out again, it nearly killed me the first time.

So now he asked me if I wanted to go to the zoo with him. I said we couldn't; it was closed. But I had another idea. I told him we should wait until tomorrow though, (or at least later today) (technically) because New Year's Eve is a really bad time to drive anywhere.

Then he asked if I wanted to go skiing New Year's Day, so I said yes. "Just like that? Yes?" He was pretty much stunned. So was I. I never say "yes" without thinking something through.

Running out of space here and will have to keep this brief. Or insert extra pages.

I picked up Grant yesterday morning, but then told him he had to drive. Not having much luck lately in that department, why risk it?

"We're taking this car. Into the mountains?" He gave the Bull a disparaging look.

"I know, I know, it's hideous and skids easily. But it does have a ski rack," I pointed out.

We went to Breckenridge and skied and boarded. So much fun, I couldn't believe it, like I hadn't really been outside in months. Of course, I hadn't. Really. Unless you count commuting and driving, being stuck in hailstorms and snowdrifts. We only skied for a few hours, but it felt great.

New Year's Resolution: Cut back on hours at work. Add hours outdoors. Break it to Gerry gently, though.

After skiing we were driving back on I-70 and I made Grant stop to see the buffalo.

Resolution Two: Organize school event involving saving more buffalo in the wild. Perhaps free the buffalo at the Denver Zoo. Which reminded me.

"I still want to see the polar bears," I said. "It isn't that far out of the way, right?" Actually it was quite a few miles away from our neighborhood, but I didn't want the day to end.

We were there at 4:00 when the sky got dark and they

turned the holiday lights on; it's this thing they do every year, and you walk through and see all these cool light displays in the shapes of animals. Tonight was the final night—they held it over longer than usual because the weather has been so unusually crappy lately and people had stayed home. And they turned the lights on early so you could see lights plus animals. Perfect.

First we went to the Northern Shores area, where all the Arctic animals are. We still had our skiing clothes on so we looked sort of Arctic ourselves. We checked out the polar bears right off. Two little ones were walking around the display, and the mother was swimming.

Every time I said something about them, from what I'd learned on TV, Grant would say something, too. Like we'd watched all the same shows. And we both knew they were only a pound or two when they were born and that they make a loud noise like bees buzzing when they nurse and how their fur is hollow like straw and that the adults don't eat for several months every year while they're waiting for Hudson Bay to freeze up so they can walk on it.

I was so excited to be there with someone who actually *got it*. Who cared. The cubs started playing, and I grabbed Grant's arm.

Then he put his hand over my hand. I was getting really nervous, I was afraid the polar bears would sense it and freak out.

"Come on, let's go see something else," I said, dragging Grant away.

"Okay . . ." he said.

We were going down this path admiring more of the lights when we saw the biggest light of all, this giant giraffe, towering into the sky. And who was sitting at the bottom of it, gazing up at it, looking forlorn?

OSCAR!!!!!!!!!

Grant talked to him nicely, in this quiet voice, very calm—like that guy who whispers to horses. He got close enough to pet Oscar on the head, then he grabbed his neck—gently, of course. We got him! Once Oscar knew it was us he jumped up on me and licked my face.

I was so happy I threw my arms around him and kissed him.

Not Oscar this time—Grant. He looks a lot more huggable these days.

He kissed me back. He kept kissing me. And it felt incredible. And I didn't even have my pager on.

We walked to the car sort of hugging, our arms around each other, with Oscar trotting between us. I kept wondering how Oscar ended up way over here, and Grant asked if we ever lived near here, and I said no. And how come he hadn't been picked up by the zoo? What if he got into a fight with an exotic animal?

"It's Oscar," Grant said. "I'm sure he ran away whenever anyone tried to catch him—animal or human."

"They could have used a tranquilizer dart!" I said.

"He's a dog, Courtney. And let's face it, people care a lot more about exotic animals than they do about plain old dogs like Oscar." He started going on and on about how when he becomes a vet, he's going to spend all his time and money on educating people on how to treat their pets, he has horror stories from working at Pet Me blah blah blah.

It was all fascinating, and I agreed with him a hundred percent and admired him even more than before. But I wanted to get back to making out.

So, okay. I only have one page left. And I know I said I wouldn't go out with any guys this year, that I pledged this back in September. And it might seem like I broke my pledge. A little bit.

But if you think about it, technically I did make it through "the year" without dating. You know—because I didn't say I meant the academic year. I meant until the end of the *calendar* year, and this is a new year, right?

Oh wait. I just found my old floral diary where I made that so-called pledge. I did say something about not dating anyone "senior year."

Who cares?

I'll just rename the next several months precollege-freshman year.

That is, if I get into a college.

If I don't end up being the poster girl for Truth or Dairy.

Which reminds me. I'm late for work. Gerry's going to give me another motivational speech about promptness being related to smoothieness, and I don't think I can stand listening to that again. I'd better go.

Resolution Three: Never be late to work again.

I hope WWW comes in today. When she reminds me

to have safe sex, I will just say yes with a smile. Maybe give her an extra wheatgrass punch on her card.

Resolution Four: Go to First National Blanks on the way home from work and pick out a new journal. Am ending this one just when things are getting (more) interesting.

SOMETIMES LOVE IS LIKE A ROCKY ROAD TRIP

8/18 FRIDAY NIGHT

Can I explain the weirdness that is my life right now?

My new college roommate, the person I have to spend the next 9 months living with, Mary Jo Johannsen, is sleeping now. Went to bed at 10. Set alarm for 5 but said she'd probably wake up before it went off. What? Who wakes up before 5?

Her straw-blond hair is spread out on the pillow. She has baby-blue flannel pajamas with little black-and-white Holstein cows on them. Which she is wearing even though it is about 90 degrees in our room.

Mary Jo is the type of person you might hate if she weren't so nice. Too nice, actually. Highly suspect. Has perfect body, perfect hair, and no clue of this. Wears unflattering clothes that end up looking good anyway. She's tan, she has muscles. She looks healthy, strong, *normal*. Sort of like Drew Barrymore.

Me, I feel like the heifer in the photo at the end of her bed. Could be the fact I ate cheese in addition to sour cream today, however. In spite of being a vegan. Okay, a semi-vegan. Mary Jo's mom brought snacks and sandwiches and cubed cheese and kept insisting I have some, wouldn't take no for an answer. Realized I had to take something or she would never stop asking. Opted for the lesser of 27 evils and had cheddar cubes.

What was I thinking when I decided to go away to college? What was I thinking when I said, "Hey, okay, Wisconsin!" I even went for a tour, which should have given me time to think. But no. Must have been in a dairy-induced daze. Just because they served free Starbucks Frappuccinos on the plane and got my vegan/vegetarian/non-chicken meal right, I took that as a sign. I make a major life decision based on that? Am I *that* insane?

Anyway, that's beside the point. It's all beside the point. The point is that I am here at Cornwall Falls College.

Mary Jo is from a small town about two hours from here. She's going to study science and math, and she likes country-western music. I'm living with a brainy Faith Hill. Who goes to bed way earlier than me and snores, I just found out a minute ago.

It's so strange, because they did make us fill out those really long questionnaires. There are like 2,000 other students here, and Mary Jo and I are supposed to be the most compatible out of all the other people I could have been matched with? Based on what? The fact we're both 18?

I am looking around our room. It is as polarized as a

plug-in. Her side: country. My side: rock 'n' roll. Her side: cows. My side: leave cows alone.

She put about 18 different editions of *Chicken Soup for the Soul* on her new dad-installed bookshelves (he built me some, too, which is very cool). What is the deal with those books? Souls don't need *soup*. And chicken? Definitely not. My soul wants miso soup, if anything.

Also, my soul wants to get out of here and move back home. To be with Grant. But I guess it's too soon to bail. When *would* be a good time? Must check Leann Rimes calendar.

Did I mention the worst part of the trip out here? When we were driving through Nebraska, I saw this evil road sign on the highway: "Exit 126. Ogallala. Grant."

Total conspiracy to make me burst out crying and regret decision to be in a mini-van leaving Grant behind. "They should really put more thought into those signs," I told Mom. "It's not very considerate of them."

"It's a town, Courtney," Mom said. "Grant's been here for years and years. It's not a conspiracy."

Sure it isn't. That town's name never *used* to be on the sign, okay?

Then we had to drive through Grant County when we got to Wisconsin. And then I studied the map and realized there is also a Superior, WI, way up north. This is in addition to Grant and Superior in Colorado.

Grant Superior is everywhere. Just not here with me, where he should be.

Mom just left, caravanning in Caravan behind Grandpa and Grandma and giant trailer, which Grandma and Grandpa and Mom all slept in last night, in the dorm parking lot. Completely embarrassing when they marched upstairs this morning with towels around their necks, ready for showers. I love her and them. I do. But I was dying for a second of time by myself. All day yesterday, Mom wouldn't stop talking.

"I know you miss Grant. How about we get some nice, crisp, tart apples and some nice Wisconsin cheddar," she suggested.

How would that fix anything? She *knows* I don't eat cheese.

"Mom, *no*," I said. I was talking about the "nice" cheddar, but she thought I was rebuffing her in general and got upset. Then I had to make it up to her by being extra nice the rest of the day. If I were a cheddar, I'd be an extra sharp.

I haven't been in the state for even 48 hours and I'm already using cheese terms to describe myself.

I've got to talk to Grant.

Just tried calling him. Grant is not home. How can he not be home? I need him.

This is going to suck, isn't it?

LATER . . .

Just discovered that Mary Jo's mini-fridge is not

stocked with soda, as I hoped. The thing is packed full of meat and cheese. It's like a deli case.

So I got a glass of water from the drinking fountain. But you know what? Even the water here tastes like milk. It's like some science fiction universe. A World Made Entirely of Milk. The question is not "Got milk?" but rather, "Got anything *but* milk?" I honestly don't think I can make it here.

Tried to be optimistic. Decided to decorate my side of the room. I put up my animal rights poster. It looks sort of strange next to the picture of Mary Jo from 4-H showing her champion cow Sophie, which is next to the photo of her gold-medal goat Chipper, but, oh well.

Then I hung up my favorite pictures of Grant, and me and Grant. And me and Beth and Jane. And Grant. Pretty soon I had this major collage going, so I finished it.

Then R.A., Krystyne (yes, that's how she spells it), walked by and saw me holding the glue gun. "Uff da!" she yelled.

"Um . . . what?" I said. "Is that a compliment?"

"No, it's Norwegian for 'Whoa, Courtney!'" She started laughing. She was really cracking herself up. "What did you do? You're not supposed to use that stuff. It's a fire hazard." She said glue wasn't on the list of "approved mounting materials" (what?!). So I had to take down all the photos. She said I had to get a bulletin board, and that they sold some really nice ones at the bookstore.

I was so mad. All the work I'd done. I was just trying to make this place look like mine. And the pictures were already stuck to the wall; they didn't come off easily. I got so frustrated, I just yanked at one. I ripped in half one of the pictures of me and Grant with our arms around each other.

NOT AN OMEN NOT AN OMEN NOT AN OMEN

I grabbed the Scotch tape and put about 6 layers on. You can't even tell it's me and Grant anymore.

NOT AN OMEN NOT AN OMEN NOT AN OMEN

Need to e-mail Grant now and ask him to send more pictures of us.

8/21 ...

Just had our first official 3rd floor meeting. It was called "The Settling-In Shindig," and was supposedly happening on every floor of every dorm here tonight at the same time. Eerie. Freaky Friday. Except it's Monday.

At the meeting, R.A. Krystyne made us all sit in a circle, introduce ourselves, and say something about what we did over the summer and why we chose to come to Cornwall Falls—what influenced our decisions.

"I worked at this smoothie and ice cream café called Truth or Dairy, and I came here due to temporary insanity," were my comments.

Everyone laughed and then Krystyne said, "No, *really*, Courtney."

6

Really. It's true, I wanted to say. But I came up with something about how I wanted to explore the world beyond in order to better understand the universe. Sounded sort of astronaut-like. Courtney In Space.

After we all introduced ourselves, there was a talk from the student health service about not doing drugs and about having safe sex. Like we haven't had the same talk since 6ᵗʰ grade, or 2ⁿᵈ, or whenever it was they started badgering us. It went pretty quickly because nobody asked any questions. Nobody *had* any questions.

Afterward, we all dispersed and went back to our rooms. Which was good because I wanted to finish my package for Grant.

"What are you doing?" Mary Jo asked when I started filling an envelope with a bunch of different things for Grant: a goofy postcard of a cheese factory, a copy of my class schedule, a list of things that seemed weird about Mary Jo. Like the fact she used health and beauty products originally intended for horses or cows. (Grant would probably know all about them: Mane 'n Tail? Udder Butter? Bag Balm? Am I living with a girl or a thoroughbred?) I use stuff not tested on animals. She uses stuff *created for* animals. Which means they have to test it on them, don't they? How can you tell if a horse shampoo is bad, anyway? If its tail has split ends?

"I'm putting together a letter for Grant," I told Mary Jo. "My boyfriend, remember?"

"Tell me more about Grant," she said. "What's he like?"

I just sat there and stared at all the pictures of him on the bulletin board. "He's great."

"He's really good-looking," she said. "Are you going to get married?"

"What? I don't know!" I laughed. "How would I know that? I'm only eighteen."

Mary Jo shrugged. "Most people back home know. My parents got married when *they* were eighteen."

"Oh. Well, see . . . mine didn't," I said. I actually didn't know how old they were, off the top of my head, but I did know they hadn't *stayed* married. Which reminded me. Dad was way behind with his monthly check.

I started writing another letter. *Dear Dad . . . Hello? Do you expect me to live on Saltines and tap water?*

"So, um, do you and Grant have a commitment?" Mary Jo asked. "Like a promise ring?"

"What? No." I did, however, have the faux rabies tag necklace, which was almost the same thing. And he bought me a new hoop for my belly button, and if that isn't commitment I don't know what is.

"Oh. So you're not serious," Mary Jo said.

"Yes we are!" I protested. What was her problem? "We're *extremely* serious. But we've only been together for about nine months."

Getting engaged at 18? I mean, I love Grant and all. But that really hadn't crossed my mind. Should it have? Am I weird for not thinking about it? Does Grant think about it?

Don't miss any of these must-reads by Catherine Clark!

Better Latte Than Never

This is not how Peggy Fleming Farrell planned to spend her summer—being the barista in a gas station coffee shop. But she's sure that she can turn the summer around if she could only get a certain waiter to look her way.

Banana Splitsville

When Courtney's boyfriend breaks up with her she decides to make senior year boy-free. But can she really give up guys? Or will her friend Grant change her mind about everything?

Rocky Road Trip

Courtney survived senior year in *Banana Splitsville*. But at college with her boyfriend 1,000 miles away, only one thing is certain: Long-distance romance is a bumpy road.

Picture Perfect

On the beaches of the Outer Banks, North Carolina, Emily meets a way-too-photogenic guy, and her picture-perfect summer starts developing quickly. Will this one be *Prints* Charming?

Icing on the Lake

Kirsten's New Year's resolution is to find a hockey-playing, winter-loving hottie to invite to her weekend cabin. No problem...right?

Maine Squeeze

Living on a tiny island off the coast of Maine is boring, right? Not when you have a great new boyfriend...and then last summer's boyfriend unexpectedly comes to town!

So Inn Love

Liza has finally landed her dream job at the Tides Inn on the Rhode Island shore. Now she just needs to figure out a way to get in with the in crowd.

Wish You Were Here

Ariel is stuck on an "America's Heartland" bus tour with her family for four weeks! But then she meets intriguing, also-miserable Andre. Who has a plan to escape.

HARPER TEEN
An Imprint of HarperCollins Publishers
www.harperteen.com